Urn Burial

A
Phryne Fisher
Mystery

Kerry Greenwood

Constable • London

CONSTABLE

First published in Australia in 1996 by Penguin Books, Australia
First published by Allen & Unwin, Australia, in 2003

This edition published in Great Britain in 2015 by Constable
1 3 5 7 9 10 8 6 4 2

A CIP catalogue record for this book
is available from the British Library.

ISBN 978-1-47211-661-1 (paperback)
ISBN: 978-1-47211-675-8 (ebook)

Typeset in Bembo by TW Typesetting, Plymouth, Devon
Printed and bound in Great Britain by CPI Group (UK) Ltd, Croydon, CR0 4YY

Constable
is an imprint of
Constable & Robinson Ltd
100 Victoria Embankment
London EC4Y 0D

An Hachette UK Company
www.hachette.co.uk

www.littlebrown.co.uk

This book is dedicated to my sister Amanda Butcher, dear Sam.

ACKNOWLEDGEMENTS

With thanks to Jean Greenwood, Lesley Greagg, Jenny Pausacker, David Greagg, Richard Revill, the staff and students of Lowther Hall, Susan Tonkin as always, my Sisters in Crime and Agatha Christie. Also AWG for the Beretta, John Russell for the hat and Corrie and Garry de Klijn for the lamp.

In loving memory of Tom (The Comm) Hills, most courageous of red-raggers and most honoured comrade.

NOTE: Buchan Caves are as described, but the named caves were closed some years ago because of environmental degradation.

CAST LIST

TOM REYNOLDS, a publisher, owner of Cave House.

EVELYN REYNOLDS, his wife.

THE HON. PHRYNE FISHER, an amazing woman.

MISS DOROTHY (DOT) WILLIAMS, her maid and companion.

MR LIN CHUNG, Phryne's lover.

MR LI PEN, his manservant and bodyguard.

MAJOR WILLIAM LUTTRELL, a military bully.

MRS LETTY LUTTRELL, his faded and frightened wife.

MISS CYNTHIA MEDENHAM, a novelist and Vamp.

MR GERALD RANDALL, a young flannelled fool, slim with curly dark hair.

MR JACK LUCAS, another, but taller and blond.

MISS JUDITH FLETCHER, a hearty young damsel, brought as a mate for Gerald by Joan Fletcher.

MRS JOAN FLETCHER, a society dame with lots of money.

DOCTOR GEORGE FRANKLIN, a fashionable practitioner with nerve trouble.

MISS SAPPHIRA CRAY, devoted to good works, a knitting friend of Miss Mead.

MISS MARY MEAD, a spinster.

MR TADEUSZ LODZ, a Polish poet.

STAFF

MR JOHN JONES, the houseman.

MR PAUL BLACK, the mechanic and driver.

MISS LINA WRIGHT, the parlourmaid.

MRS DAISY CROFT, the cook.

MR ALBERT HINCHCLIFF, the butler.

MRS BELINDA HINCHCLIFF, the housekeeper.

MR TERENCE WILLIS, the stableman.

DINGO HARRY, a wandering and extremely eccentric swagman who knows all about the caves.

DOREEN, the chambermaid.

ANNIE, the housemaid.

A scullery maid, two gardeners, a knives and boots boy called albert and a stableman's apprentice called joe.

'But man is a noble animal, splendid in ashes, and pompous in the grave, solemnizing nativities and deaths with equal lustre, nor omitting ceremonies of bravery in the infamy of his nature.'

Urn Burial, Sir Thomas Browne, Chapter V.

CHAPTER ONE

We present not these as any strange sights or spectacle
unknown to your eyes, who have beheld the best of
urns and the noblest variety of ashes.

Epistle Dedicatory, *Urn Burial*, Sir Thomas Browne.

THE SHOT boomed out of the mist.

Phryne slowed the Hispano-Suiza to a halt. Dot,
from the back, where she was sitting with Lin
Chung's manservant Li Pen, said tremulously,
'Someone hunting?'

'In this weather and after dark?' asked Phryne.
'Does that seem likely, Dot dear? That was a
shotgun.'

Then someone screamed.

It was a female voice, ragged with terror, even
though the sound was blanketed by the fog which
curled into the big car, chilling the heart. Li Pen
leaned forward. Dot emitted a squeak of fright.

'What do you want to do?' asked Lin Chung. 'It
might be a private fight.'

Phryne grinned at him. 'The last private fight I leapt into was very rewarding,' she commented. 'I would otherwise never have met you. Can you use a gun?'

'Not as well as you, I suspect.'

'All right, change places. You take the driver's seat.' She clambered over him, taking the passenger seat. The scream came again, closer and louder, and Phryne heard feet running. Dot whimpered. Li Pen, hoping he was doing the right thing, put a reassuring hand on her arm, which she was too frightened to shake off.

Phryne found her Beretta and loaded it methodically. Lin Chung heard the click of bullets snapped into their grooves, and the clunk of the mechanism as she closed it.

'Turn the car until the headlights point directly behind me,' she ordered. 'That should blind anyone coming this way. Keep the engine running – I won't be a tick.'

She was gone from beside him. Lin engaged the gears and very carefully and skilfully backed the Hispano-Suiza and turned it, hoping that he was not about to run Phryne's beloved car into an unexpected ditch. The powerful fog lamps outlined Phryne's small determined figure; the slim body clad in trousers and a jumper, her stance easy and alert, and the cameo-cut shape of her straight profile and cap of black hair. Li Pen commented in Cantonese, 'She would make a warrior. She has the heart of a lion.' Lin Chung agreed.

'Oh, Miss, be careful!' wailed Dot.

The road was rough. Three-foot high ti-tree scrub lined it, full of thorns and snakes. Phryne called into the mist, 'Here!' and for a moment there was complete silence. Chill as the heart of darkness, thought Lin Chung, his hands ready on the wheel. Cold as the silence at the heart of unbeing.

Scarves of fog lay tangled in the low-growing scrub. Phryne strained her eyes. She could see only about ten paces into the virgin forest and could smell only wetness and chill earth and the faint scent of water. Then she heard a crashing scramble straight ahead as someone tried to run through the ti-tree.

This, of course, could not be done. Only a bull-dozer could run through there, she reflected, holding the gun out steady in both hands. 'Here!' she yelled again, and was answered by a sobbing shriek, 'Help!'

Out of the fog came a woman, completely out of her mind with pain or fear, stumbling and falling as the roots caught her feet, getting up and clawing herself forward again. She staggered, fell and got up again, orienting herself by the car's headlights, drawn by the bright light like a moth.

Phryne swung her aim away as the girl fell panting at her feet. She was dressed in black and white, and a frilly cap was still pinned, jaunty and incongruous, on her torn hair. It was an unusual situation in which to find a parlourmaid.

Phryne listened hard, trying to block out the maid's whimpering, trying to hear beyond the sound for any following feet. The attacker must still be out there. Phryne and the maid were perfect targets in the Hispano-Suiza's glare. But nothing moved, no gun fired. She could discern no other person out in the chill darkness.

'Come along,' she said, pocketing the gun and hauling the girl to her feet. 'Get in the car. You're safe now. Lin, get us out of here,' she added, shoving the maid into the back seat and Dot's concerned arms.

The parlourmaid's sobbing increased once she knew she was safe. Li Pen removed himself to the far side of the seat as she caught sight of his face and whispered, 'A Chink!'

'You're safe,' said Dot briskly. 'It's all right. What's your name? Where did you come from? Where can we take you?'

'Lina,' whispered the girl. 'I'm Lina and I'm from Cave House.'

Dot soothed, 'Good, that's where we're going.'

Lin Chung, navigating carefully through endless ti-tree, said, 'It can't be far, then.'

'Oh, God, another Chink!' exclaimed Lina as she heard his voice.

'Lina, would you like to walk home?' asked Phryne, her voice as chill as the fog.

Dot said, 'Oh, Miss . . .' and the parlourmaid gave a small scream. 'No Miss, please Miss, I'm sorry . . .'

'It's Miss Phryne Fisher,' said Dot, giving the girl a small shake. 'We're going to Cave House for a house party. Mr Reynolds invited us. I'm Miss

Williams and that is Mr Lin and Mr Li. Pull your-self together, girl. You've been rescued and we're taking you home. You were lucky that we came along. No call to be insulting your Master's guests now, have you? Are you hurt? We heard a shot.'

'No – no, he missed me, I'm just a bit scratched by all them thorns. I was so scared. I'm sorry, Miss Fisher, Mr Lin, I'm sorry.' She started to cry. Phryne was unsympathetic.

Lin Chung said softly, 'You see, Phryne, I told you this would be difficult, importing an exotic like me into your world. She's just reacting as all the rest will.'

'She's shocked and she's been reading too much Sax Rohmer,' snapped Phryne. 'At last – they look like the gateposts.'

'Yes, Miss. It says "Cave House" on the fence,' Dot said, supporting the sobbing girl on her shoulder and feeling tears trickle down her neck. Phryne got out to open the gate and the car rolled onto a gravelled drive. She snibbed the wooden stockyard shutter after the car had passed through and listened again.

No sound in the dank air, yet she shivered. Someone was watching her. There were inimical eyes on the back of her neck. She pulled up the collar of her jumper and got back into the car.

Even the fog could not disguise the monstrous oddity of Cave House.

In the closing years of the nineteenth century, a wealthy brewer had been dragged protesting on the Grand Tour by his wife, who had artistic yearnings. There was no doubt that they had visited Greece, and also delighted in a profusion of Gothic cathedrals. Cave House was both. It was an amalgam so outrageous, so amazing, that even Phryne, in possession of a distraught housemaid and a searing fit of bad temper, sat and gaped.

The Parthenon, she recalled, had nine columns with decorous Ionic capitals. Cave House had twelve and they were capped with Corinthian designs in white marble. York Cathedral had ten Gothic grotesques over the door; Cave House had twenty, all fanged and with unpleasantly lolling tongues as well.

It was too much for the end of a long drive. Lin Chung sat as though stunned, every canon of design known to him, both Chinese and Oxford, thoroughly outraged. Li Pen reflected that even the legendary Yellow Emperor on an overdose of hallucinogenic mushrooms had never conceived anything like this. Dot thought it was overdone, but interesting.

'Miss, we ought to get Lina inside,' she said, and Phryne pulled herself together. Artistic criticism of Cave House could wait. Now she was cold and furious and needed to suitably dispose of Lina, who was working herself into a proper fit of hysterics by the sounds from the back seat.

The main door opened and Tom Reynolds himself came out.

He was short, stout and hearty, and ordinarily Phryne liked him. At this moment she didn't like anyone.

'Well, what a terrible night for a drive!' he exclaimed. 'Come inside instantly! John will put the car away. Phryne dear, you must be chilled to the bone. I'd quite given you up!'

'The fog slowed us down.' Phryne got out and climbed up the steps to kiss Tom on the cheek. 'Also, we've found a stray of yours, Tom.'

Dot helped the parlourmaid from the car. Reynolds identified her and goggled.

'Lina? What have you been up to?'

The maid began to shriek again. Dot put an arm around her.

'Have you got a housekeeper, Sir?' she asked. 'Pipe down, Lina, do. You'll soon be inside. Sir, I think we'd better call a doctor.'

'Yes, of course. Take her inside, through to the kitchen. I'll send Mrs Hinchcliff to you right away, and Doctor Franklin's staying in the house. What a stroke of luck.'

Two housemen were unloading the luggage, and Phryne allowed them to take the car away.

'Mr Lin, delighted to meet you. I've heard a lot about you,' effused Tom Reynolds, shaking his hand.

Dot and Li Pen escorted Lina into the house through the front door, ordinarily banned to domestics. Phryne saw the girl's knees give way abruptly. Li Pen swept her up and carried her and Phryne reflected that he was a lot stronger than he looked. Then again, so was Lin Chung. Tom Reynolds was drawing them inside, past the great carved portals and into a proper cathedral entrance.

'The maid'll show you to your rooms, and perhaps you'd like to come down in about half an hour for a drink and some supper, eh? It's ten o'clock and we keep early hours in the country.' Phryne assented absently, boggling.

The inside of Cave House was as remarkable as the outside.

Following a neat maid, Phryne crossed a parquet floor with Greek key-pattern edging, climbed up a monumental staircase under some Morris windows and paced along a gallery to a large room. Lin Chung had been led in exactly the opposite direction to some distant bit of the house. Phryne scented prejudice.

But the room was very pleasant. There was a bright fire burning in the black-leaded hearth under the *Art Décoratif* tiles and the Corinthian columns of the marble mantelpiece. Her bed was four-posted, surrounded by white mosquito netting, and had a thick feather quilt. The floor was covered with a hideous but expensive Turkish carpet in glaring red and brilliant green. Phryne took stock. Her room had two bow windows; a powdering closet with a small bed in it, obviously intended for Dot, a lot of exceptionally miscellaneous furniture and an engraving of *Hope* over her washstand. Hope, as a draped female figure, drooped over the globe of the world, obviously in irreparable, mortal despair at the pitiless nature of mankind. It was an exceptionally depressing picture.

Irritated, Phryne turned her to the wall. Then

she tore off her hat, unlaced her boots, and sat down on a spindly Louis Quatorze chair at a marble washstand. Her face in the mirror was set with fury. And, she noticed, smudged. She poured some hot water into a Wedgewood bowl and washed the marks of adventure off her skin with Pear's soap.

She was sitting by the fire and wiggling some feeling back into her frozen toes when Dot came in.

'How's Lina?' asked Phryne.

'The Doctor's with her. He says she's all right, just exhausted and scratched by all those thorns but he says . . . oh, Miss.'

'Oh, Miss? What's the matter, old thing? Sit down, Dot, have a tot of this.'

Dot slumped down into the chippendale chair on the other side of the fire. Phryne produced a flask and made her companion drink down a mouthful of brandy. Some colour came back into Dot's white face. Phryne took her hand, worried by her pallor. Finally Dot managed to say what was on her mind.

'She's been molested, Miss.'

'God, you mean raped?'

Dot winced at the word. 'No, Miss Phryne, just molested. The Doctor says she'll be all right. The housekeeper's with her – her aunt, she says. Mr Li carried her in, and he's gone to find Mr Lin. They've put him right out the back.'

'Yes, as far away from me as possible. I suspect either moralism or racism, Dot, which I would not have expected from an old reprobate like Tom. God, that poor girl, and I was so angry with her. Oh well, can't be helped.' Phryne dismissed the thought. 'I'll go and see her tomorrow.'

'She's just saying what everyone says, Miss. And you were right. Her aunt says she's always reading Fu Manchu.'

Phryne laughed. 'And what do you think of Lin Chung, Dot?'

'I never met any Chinese people before, Miss,' said Dot slowly, stretching out her hands to the fire, 'so I never thought about them. Then he came along and he's so educated, so *soigné*,' (she produced the French word with pride) 'that I never thought of him as Chinese, Miss. He's just himself. He's a nice man. The girls like him, he talks to them and he's taught them that satin stitch from China. Never drunk, never loud – the butlers think he's an ornament to the house, Miss Phryne, that's what Mrs B said. And that Mr Li, he's nice, too. He was real good with Lina. She woke up while he was carrying her and screamed again and he didn't even drop her. He's awful strong for his size. Lina thinks the Chows are out to get her and sell her for a white slave. I don't think she's very bright, Miss.'

'Bright or not, she's had a dreadful experience. I wonder who the man with the shotgun was? They play nasty games in the country, Dot. We must decline to join in these rural frolics. There, get into a dressing gown, Dot dear, get warm. Your bones must be chilled. You can have first bath, it's just down the hall. I'm going down for a late supper with Tom, and a little *éclaircissement* about Lin Chung into the bargain. Shall I get them to send a tray up for you?'

'No, Miss, I'll just have a warm-up and change into a dress and then go down to the kitchen. Mrs Croft's making Mr Li and me some supper. I'm all right, Miss, really. It's just – out in the car . . .'

'Mmm?' Phryne had pulled off her jumper and was rummaging for another in her trunk.

'I could feel eyes, Miss, eyes in the dark. I mean, I thought I could. I was probably just imagining it.'

Phryne, half-clad, came to lay a hand on her maid's shoulders and look into the troubled brown eyes.

'No, Dot dear, you weren't imagining it, or if you were I was imagining it, too. There was someone out in the dark, watching us arrive. Probably Lina's attacker, who is armed with a shotgun, and who didn't like us – not one bit. I was immediately reminded of a Kenyan wait-a-bit hide, the hunter and I sat there all night once, watching the waterhole for a man-eating lion – and all the time he was behind us, glaring at my back. When I got out to close the gate I had just that sense of a predator marking me down for prey. Oh well, there is safety in numbers. You stick close to Li Pen if we come to any real danger, Dot dear, which of course, we won't. I suspect that Li could be very useful in a crisis. And this is probably some bucolic loony whom everyone will instantly know and identify and they'll take him right away to a nice safe jail. Don't worry about it, Dot,' she advised, finding and donning a red velvet evening top and slipping her feet into soft shoes. 'Now get warm and have some supper. I won't be long.'

Phryne descended the monumental staircase and found her host in the parlour where a nice little supper for three was laid out in front of the fire. Phryne took a Sheridan chair and accepted a glass of sherry.

She examined her host. Tom looked uncomfortable, which did not suit him. His charm had always been his raffish indolence; now concern folded his face into unfamiliar lines.

'Well, Phryne my dear, you're here at last.' His voice was an echo of his usual heartiness. Phryne looked him in the eye and he shifted to avoid her gaze.

'Yes, and I have a problem,' she said directly. 'Why is Lin Chung placed so far away from me? Are you developing moral scruples, Tom?'

'Not me.' He disclaimed morality and took a gulp of his sherry. 'My wife felt that . . .'

'Oh, yes? I haven't met her, have I?'

'No, she's a wonderful woman, wonderful, but she has her . . . prejudices.'

'And one of them is that she doesn't like Chinese.'

'Yes. But anyway, you have to think of your reputation, Phryne. You're always skating on the edge of social ruin. This affair could . . .'

'Tip me over? I don't think so. I'm an Hon. and I'm rich – they need me a good deal more than I need them. I tell you, Tom, I object very strenuously to this attempt to censor my behaviour.'

Tom reflected that even hungry, tired and furious, the Honourable Phryne Fisher was beautiful. Her green eyes flashed in her pale face and he found himself wishing he were ten years younger and three stone lighter. That Chinese was a lucky blighter.

'Well, well, you will do as you like, I expect. You'll meet Evelyn at breakfast. She's a little conservative, but I'm sure you'll like each other.'

'I'm sure,' lied Phryne.

Lin Chung, who had been halted by the mention of his name outside the door, came in as Phryne said, 'How is Lina?'

'Doctor Franklin says she's just bruised, chilled and shocked. He's given her something to make her sleep. Though what would have become of her if you hadn't happened along, Phryne, Mr Lin, I don't know. There's nothing around here until you come to Buchan Caves, and that's a good couple of miles across difficult country.' He chuckled. 'She says she saw your headlights and ran for them, so she's all bumped and scratched but her virtue is intact. One of these rural wooings, I expect, that went a bit far.'

'No, Tom, it wasn't like that,' Phryne began.

'Just a bit of slap and tickle in the moonlight,' said Tom. 'Have some soup, Mr Lin. It's chicken.'

Phryne said flatly, 'Tom, that girl was terrified for her life, not her virtue, and I heard a gun fired. And tonight is not a night that even the most determined and lustful rustic wooer would choose for an assignation. It's as cold as the grave.'

'Never deterred me,' said Tom. 'Not with a good compliant parlourmaid in prospect. Ah, that was a long time ago. Would you like soup, Phryne? Yes? I expect the girl heard someone out after rabbits and got a fright. Nothing to be alarmed about.'

Phryne gave it up, accepted a bowl of very good soup, and then a slice of cold roast beef on home-made bread. Lin Chung offered a few suitable words about the house, about which Phryne felt the less said, the better.

After supper, Lin Chung escorted her to the head of the staircase where she detained him with a hand on his arm.

'Thank you for your support tonight,' she said. 'You drive very well.'

The bronze face inclined gravely. 'It was my pleasure, Silver Lady.'

'Do you know where my room is?'

'Yes, but I shall deny myself that honour.'

'Oh?' Phryne could not believe her ears. 'Why?'

'Your reputation, Phryne. I overheard Mr Reynolds just now. An affair with a Chinese is social ruin, he said. He is probably correct. While that remains the case, I would do nothing to injure you.'

'Hmm.' Phryne did not have an immediate

counter-argument. This needed thinking about and she was tired and worried by Tom's refusal to take the attack on his employee seriously. 'Very well. I'll see you at breakfast. Sleep well.'

'Ah, Silver Lady,' he whispered, so that she could only hear him by standing close, 'not as well as I would with you.'

Phryne breathed in the cool scent of his skin for a moment, then kissed him decorously on the cheek and walked to her room, without looking back.

CHAPTER TWO

We were hinted by the occasion, not catched the opportunity to write of old things, or intrude upon the antiquary. We are coldly drawn unto the discourses of antiquities, who have scarce time to comprehend new things, or make out learned novelties.

Epistle Dedicatory, *Urn Burial*, Sir Thomas Browne.

BREAKFAST WAS early; Phryne arrived at nine o'clock and found that most of the guests had eaten and gone. This was all to the good. She had slept well but alone, and that never improved her temper. She had only one companion: a youngish man with a very self-conscious tie and long straight dark-brown hair falling over his face, who was eating as though he did not expect to ever see bacon and eggs again – the famous surrealist poet, Tadeusz Lodz, whom she recognised at once. He was good-looking in an unwashed bohemian fashion, and as soon as he saw her he laid down his cutlery, rose to his feet and bowed over her hand, which Phryne thought was courtly above the call of duty, considering how hungry he evidently was.

She poured herself a cup of coffee and gathered some toast and a poached egg from the steaming silver dishes lined up on the buffet. The coffee was cold and she rang a small silver bell for more.

A scrubbed and bouncing housemaid, cap askew, took the order and came back in a very short time with a fresh pot. Phryne drank some of the inky beverage. It was scalding and mostly composed of chicory. She grimaced. There seemed to be some sort of idea amongst Australian cooks, amounting to a religious conviction, that the combination of lukewarm water and Grocer's Best Ground constituted the drink which Parisians called *café* and wrote songs about. The poet cleared his plate, took a gulp of tea and said, 'I am delighted to meet you, Madame. Would you care for some ham – some bacon – more toast?'

His voice was delightful, a dark-brown toffee-coloured voice, with a marked accent which turned his W into a V and made his vowels lush and prolonged.

'No, nothing more, thank you. Well, perhaps a sliver of ham. Mr Lodz, may I ask you a strange question?'

'Madame?' incongruously blue eyes lit with interest.

'Did you hear a shot last night?'

'Do you know, the whole time I have been in this Australia, no one has asked me such a question. Remarkable. But I regret, Madame, I was

— 17 —

struggling with some lines which would not become absurd – they remained, no matter what I did with them, ridiculously banal – and I heard nothing. Why? Who was shot?'

'No one. A maid was attacked, though, and I certainly heard a shot.' Phryne ate her toast. 'Tell me, Mr Lodz, your natural habitat must be a cafe – I have never known a poet, especially a surrealist, to move far from his *café au lait* – what brings a town-dweller like you to the country?'

'But who else but my host? He is to publish a small book of mine, a little volume.' He made a dismissive gesture. 'Nothing really, but Reynolds brought me here to finish it. If I am in the town, I have too many good companions. I drink, I talk ... and nothing gets written. Thought, argued over, dreamed, discussed, considered, certainly – but written, no. You would know this, Madame, you who have known many poets, in Paris, perhaps? And this grotesque and delightful house is a perfect place for a surrealist – it cries out for a resident poet who can really appreciate its strangeness. Therefore, I am here. I ask the same of you. What brings so sophisticated and beautiful a lady to this rural setting, hmm?'

Phryne was wondering the same thing and enumerated her reasons over a cup of Cave House tea, which was much more palatable than the coffee.

'Tom Reynolds is an old friend of mine, my adopted daughters are back at school, the house is empty, and I need a rest. I have just concluded a nasty case at the theatre and I felt like a little holiday.'

'*Bien sûr*,' agreed the poet affably. 'Will you introduce me to your Chinese? Such a beautiful face, like a bronze. What is his name?'

'Lin Chung. They call him Lin.'

'I wish I could draw,' lamented the poet. 'Every time I see a face like that I long to be able to capture the beauty; the cool, aloof beauty in the bones.'

'Never mind. You capture it in words.'

'You are very kind.' The poet smiled, revealing a face containing unexpected humour as well as the strength of character to be seen in all surrealists. It took determination to be really strange. That, or absinthe before breakfast every day.

'So, gentle lady, a little walk, perhaps?' He held out his arm and Phryne took it.

They walked out of the breakfast room into a pillared portico lined with enough gargoyles to trouble even a surrealist. Tadeusz winced a little and guided Phryne on to a grassy path which led into a rose garden. The fog had burned away under a cool morning sun.

'A cigarette?' She accepted. He opened a battered silver case which had a tarnished outline upon it resembling a rising sun. 'They are Turkish-Balkan Sobranies which I hope are to your taste. Now, you will want to hear about the house party. You can see most of them from here.' He escorted her to a garden seat and pointed.

'There, playing at being civilised, is Major

Luttrell – a military bully, a King Boar, I assure you, beautiful lady, along with his much-tried wife.'

She saw a tall stout gentleman leaning over a small figure under the beech tree. 'He leads her a dog's life,' he said flatly. 'Some women are saints.'

'Which makes some men devils. If she'd climbed on a chair and flattened him with a poker when he first began to bully, he'd be a lot more amenable and might have some respect for her,' commented Phryne.

The poet tossed back his hair and said in a faintly astonished tone, 'As the beautiful lady says. Visible at a distance because of her illuminated gown, she has a gaudy taste, is Miss Cynthia Medenham, the novelist. You have heard of her?'

'Yes, she writes symbolic, impenetrable prose, which if it wasn't so hard to understand would probably be banned. But it sells well, I gather,' said Phryne, who had given up on *Silk* after chapter three, despite the promising ingredients of a woman who was the reincarnation of an eighteenth-century courtesan, a tiger skin, and a virgin (but virile) boy.

'Hmm, yes. How much of her rather lush prose arises from personal experience I cannot – alas – say.' The poet grinned. 'Playing with a hockey ball and stick is Miss Judith Fletcher, a jolly girl in the English manner – abominable. Do not agree to play tennis with her, she will exhaust you as she exhausted me. She drinks only water, which she calls Adam's Ale in that intolerably hearty manner, and should marry a ... a farmer. Instead, her mother,' he pointed out a middle-aged lady hastening across the ground with a sunhat in her hands, 'is determined that she should marry Gerald Randall, a flannelled fool, over there.' Two young men were hitting a cricket ball between them in a rather desultory manner. One was slim and dark, the other tall and blond and both, indeed, were wearing flannel bags and jumpers. 'His friend Jack Lucas is just such another – no brains at all and no appreciation of poetry. However, Mr Gerald plays the piano, passably, unless he attempts Liszt which cannot be recommended, anyway. He is absolutely *passé*.'

'Who, Gerald?'

'Liszt,' said the poet with strong conviction. 'There is your Mr Lin with Tom Reynolds. It was brave of him to come, but braver of you to bring him.'

'No courage was involved, I assure you.' Phryne sighted a woman of steely bearing, formally dressed in a walking costume and her daytime pearls, and asked, 'Who's that?'

'Evelyn – Mrs Reynolds. She seems to be looking for someone, Madame – could it be you?'

'Probably. Excuse me, Mr Lodz. And thank you for your most illuminating lecture.'

Evelyn Reynolds caught the end of this and said, 'What have you been lecturing Miss Fisher on, Tadeusz?'

'Why, poetry,' he said with a gentle smile which should not have deceived her for a moment. 'Poetry, but of course.'

Mrs Reynolds took Phryne's hand in her small soft grasp and said expressionlessly, 'Miss Fisher, how nice to meet you. Tom's told me all about you.'

'Mrs Reynolds.' Phryne was cordial, for the moment.

'Evelyn, please. I'm sure we are going to be friends.'

'Possibly,' said Phryne. 'That depends on whether I can stay with you, Mrs Reynolds.'

'Oh? What could prevent it?'

Phryne held on to the ringed hand and smiled into the powdered face. Mrs Reynolds was good looking, with a chocolate-box prettiness which had faded into a general pleasantness. She had blue eyes, which were beginning to look rather worried. The Honourable Miss Fisher was her social catch of the season. Mrs Reynolds would be boasting about her visit for years.

'Lin Chung. I understand that you don't like Chinese,' said Phryne flatly.

'No, indeed, what can have given you that idea? I'm sure that some of them are admirable people. Look at the Chinese preachers and the missions and . . .' She dried up.

'I just want to make it perfectly clear. Lin Chung and I are a package for the present. You either get both of us or neither. If there is any doubt in your mind that you and your staff can treat him fairly and in a civilised fashion, then we are leaving today.'

Mrs Reynolds resisted for a moment. Phryne felt

the hand twitch. She was obviously weighing up what country society would say about her accommodating a Chinese who was having an affair with the much-publicised Miss Fisher against what the country would say if Miss Fisher left in a huff because Mrs Reynolds would not accommodate him. She capitulated. 'Of course, of course, Miss Fisher, naturally. You need have no fears on that score.'

'You've placed him at the very end of the house. Can you change his room?'

'Not now, Miss Fisher, I would have to move someone else. I didn't mean ... I've got a full house, I'm sorry. But there is no objection to him – none at all, I assure you.'

Phryne stared at her and believed it. There would be no further comment about her affair with Lin Chung. Now all she had to do was convince him. She took Mrs Reynolds' arm and changed the subject.

'Evelyn, you look worried. What's the matter?'

'It's Lina. I'd only say this to you, Phryne, because you rescued the girl. She's still in hysterics and can't tell us anything about what happened – every time someone asks her a question she starts to cry again.'

'She avoided actual violation, Dot said.'

'Yes, but she's been mauled about and bruised black and blue. Can you tell me what happened? Tom should have called me last night but I had a terrible headache and I went to bed early.'

Phryne told her hostess all that she could recall

of the previous evening. Evelyn sighed.

'I can't get Tom to take it seriously,' said Phryne.

'Neither can I. He just keeps chuckling on about rural lovers so I have to restrain myself from throwing a hairbrush at him.'

Phryne began to like her hostess. She herself had just refrained from throwing a full set of fire irons at the incomprehensibly obtuse Tom and his rustic romances.

'You say you heard a shot – just one?'

'Yes. I asked Mr Lodz, but he didn't hear it. He said he was writing.'

'You know what poets are.' Evelyn's face brightened. 'Such a nice man, a good guest. He's terribly amusing and speaks five languages. He hasn't got very far with his book, though. He keeps going back to poems that Tom thought were finished and altering them. Publishers have to get used to writers, I suppose.'

'And writers used to publishers. It can't be easy for either of them. Now, can I help? Can I talk to Tom again?'

'If you like, Phryne, but it won't be the least use. He doesn't *want* to take this seriously. Mrs Hinchcliff is most upset; the stores haven't come, the butcher's boy is late and I've managed to upset you, Phryne, about Mr Lin. And now the river's rising again. Oh, dear, here I am boring on about my problems. I do beg your pardon. What would you like to know? The usual, I expect. Lunch is at one, just a light meal. Dinner is at eight, evening dress if you please. If we are up late, we have supper at eleven. Are your rooms comfortable?'

'Yes, very,' said Phryne truthfully.

'Perhaps you might like to boat. There is the boathouse – it's never locked.' She indicated a small shed on the riverfront. 'But do take care. As I said, the water's rising. We are going to the caves tomorrow, that might be an agreeable outing. There's good walking that way, and I'm sure Tom will lend you a horse if you would like to ride. It's a bit too cold for bathing, though Jack and Gerry go out bravely every morning for a cold plunge. Such nice boys. Now, who haven't you met?'

Taking Phryne firmly in tow, Mrs Reynolds conducted her to another rustic seat where an old woman was crocheting. Her fingers moved like bone shuttles, so easy and automatic was the movement. It was a small garment of some kind, perhaps for a baby. The lady was dressed in a tweed skirt, sensible shoes, and a pale-blue fluffy jumper. Her long white hair was coiled into a neat bun. She looked up, her face soft and undistinguished.

'Miss Fisher?' asked an old voice. 'I'm Miss Mead, Miss Mary Mead. Delighted to meet you,' she said, summing Phryne up, from Russian leather sole to close-cut cap of black hair in one comprehensive glance. 'Are you looking for your Mr Lin? He's in the house, I believe, with Mr Reynolds.'

Miss Mead was watching Phryne's face, and seemed disappointed when she did not react. 'Too kind,' said Phryne meaninglessly, preserving her blank expression. Evelyn led her on to another old lady, this one of the acidulated sort. She was dressed entirely in black, with a skirt down to her feet and sleeves down to her wrists, collar high about her neck, and perched on her head was probably the very last rusty black bonnet in captivity.

'This is Miss Fisher, Miss Cray.'

'Did you bring the Chinese with you?' asked a sharp voice, very suddenly. 'Is he a mission boy?'

'I beg your pardon?' asked Phryne, stepping back.

'Is he a Christian?'

'Yes, I believe so. Are you?' asked Phryne gently. Miss Reynolds smelt trouble and intervened.

'Miss Sapphira Cray is one of the Church's most tireless workers. She's always collecting for the missions.'

'Is she?' asked Phryne. 'Miss Cray? I'll make a deal with you. I'll give you quite a lot of money for your mission if you never again refer to my exceptionally educated friend as a mission boy, and refrain from insulting him for the duration of our visit. Do we have a bargain?'

Miss Cray shot Phryne a sharp look, considered whether to take offence or not, decided on the side of lucre, and nodded.

Mrs Reynolds apologised as soon as they were out of earshot. 'I'm so sorry about that, but she is a very good woman. She's Tom's second cousin, never spends a shilling on herself; always wears those dreadful old clothes, and gives everything she has to the heathen.'

'Lucky heathen,' said Phryne. They stopped at the border of the lawn, where two young men had abandoned their cricket and were strolling together, smoking cigarettes and laughing. 'I've been told that they are Gerry and Jack.'

'Yes, such nice boys. So well mannered. I think Mrs Fletcher had hopes that Gerry might take to her daughter Judith. They get on well together. Gerry's the heir to the fortune, you know.'

'No, which fortune?'

'Oh, sorry, I should have explained. His great-grandfather Randall was a ship's chandler, and he sold so well and cleverly that he made a huge fortune and had his own shipping line. Then his father married American money. I think it is so nice of the Americans to have money.'

'It quite reconciles us to their accent,' agreed Phryne. Her own grandfather had married a Chicago heiress. She had introduced steam heating, Parisian clothes and liquid assets into the Fisher family, to its eternal improvement.

'Yes, but regrettably Gerry doesn't get along with his step-mama. So he's staying here until he goes to university in March – he's reading law, I believe. His friend Jack Lucas comes from a very old family, but they've got no money at all – lost it all in the Megatherium crash. Jack's going to start work as a clerk as soon as he leaves here. I feel so sorry for him, he's just as clever as Gerry, but when I asked him what he wanted to be he laughed quite bitterly and said, "It doesn't matter what I want to be, Mrs R, I'm going to be a clerk in an auction room." So sad, poor boy.'

Phryne felt a pang. She had been acquainted with the sole perpetrator of the Megatherium business, and she had let him run away to South America. Still, even if she had handed him over to the law, the investors would have lost their cash. Bobby had spent it all on infallible betting systems on horses which broke their legs as soon as they left the barrier – or even before.

'There's Miss Fletcher.'

A robust girl ran up, tossing and catching a hockey ball in one square hand. She had short yellow hair and bright blue eyes and she cried, 'Hello! You must be Miss Fisher! I saw them polishing your car – spiffing machine. Hispano-Suiza, isn't it? Massive torque you must get from those pistons. I understand it did eighty miles an hour at the Chicago Brickyard. Magnificent design.'

'Thank you. Would you care to go for a drive in her?'

'Would you – perhaps you would let me drive?' The girl's eyes lit with eagerness.

'No,' said Phryne. 'No one drives her but me. Or my staff. Sometimes. Well, we'll see,' she said kindly, as the girl seemed very disappointed.

'I know you wouldn't want to risk her,' said Miss Fletcher, 'but I can drive. Gerry lets me drive his Bentley.'

'Does he indeed?' The girl reminded Phryne of Bunji Ross. 'Do you fly, by any chance?'

'They won't let me – yet.' The strong mouth set in determined lines. 'But I shall talk them round.'

'Yes, I think you will,' said Phryne.

Mrs Reynolds led Phryne on. 'It's hard for her,' she said sympathetically. 'Her mother is ... well, a womanly woman, and poor Judith is ... well, not ...'

'A girlish girl?' Phryne asked and her hostess shook her head.

Miss Cynthia Medenham was sitting on the bench under an ash tree, chewing the end of a pencil and staring blankly at the river. She had a silk-bound blank book on her knee, half filled with scribbled notes. She was consciously decorative, clad in a long flowing robe handpainted with pea-cocks, her blond hair carelessly caught at the nape of her neck with a jewelled clasp, her blue eyes abstracted and remote. Mrs Reynolds put a finger to her lips and tiptoed past.

Someone was sitting under the beech tree; a small figure crying softly into a handkerchief. Mrs Reynolds beckoned Phryne to walk on.

'I don't know what possessed a nice girl like Letty to marry the Major. He's very brave, has lots of medals – I suppose that she was dazzled, and of course, her young man was killed on the Somme. But he's got ... an imperious nature, and poor Letty just can't cope with him. Come along, it's getting cold. There, see? The sun's going in. How about a nice cup of tea, Phryne?'

'Thank you, Evelyn.'

The parlour contained, reading from right to left, Lin Chung looking impassive, which was a bad sign, and Tom Reynolds mopping his brow. Evelyn rang the bell, ordered the tea and commented brightly, 'The river's still rising, Tom.'

'Oh, God, the river as well. Everything is conspiring, Evelyn. I tell you, the whole world is spitting on its hands and getting on with making my life difficult.'

'Now, Tom dear, don't exaggerate.'

Tom rose to his feet and bellowed, 'I'm not exaggerating! I've got a house full of guests, the housekeeping's gone to pot, the kitchen is full of sobbing maids, I've just been condescended to for half an hour by a man who knows much more about everything than I do, and now the river's rising and threatening to cut off the house so I'll be trapped here.'

'We'll be trapped, too,' said Phryne, sitting down next to Lin Chung and taking his hand. 'What have you been doing to Tom, Lin darling?'

'We were talking about porcelain,' said Lin, seeming puzzled. 'Then about ancient writings.'

'He's a little overwrought,' Mrs Reynolds apologised. 'Pay no attention. He'll be all right when he has some tea. Tom, dear.'

The publisher sank down into a chair and rubbed his face.

'Sorry, Lin, old man, I'm sure you're right about the Tang vase. And doubtless all the other things will be fixed. But it's too much, Evie, Mrs Hinchcliff has given her notice. That means we'll lose Hinchcliff as well as Lina, and what will we do for staff?'

Phryne nodded towards the door and she and Lin Chung left unobtrusively.

'This is the strangest household,' she commented. 'Come for a walk?'

He followed her into the rose garden. It was too early for buds, but leaves were beginning to sprout.

'You look very beautiful against that shiny background,' he said. 'It's the same gloss as your hair – like very fine silk floss, such as is ordered by clerics to embroider altarcloths. I fear that I have offended our host.'

'No, he's overwrought, as his wife says. Can you ride, Lin?'

'Mostly without falling off.'

'Come on, then. We'll see what's in the stable.'

The stable yielded two hacks, thoroughbreds, well-fed and under-exercised. Lin caught and saddled his choice, a docile-looking brown mare. Phryne slid a bridle over the proud nose of a touchy gelding who danced uncooperatively as the stable-man saddled him.

'He's a tearaway is Cuba,' advised the groom. 'You watch his tricks, Miss.'

'I'll watch,' she said, putting one toe into the stirrup and hopping as Cuba shifted. She feinted, he stood still, and she swung up into the saddle.

'Fooled you,' she told him, and Cuba laid his ears back and walked reluctantly to the gate.

'Out along the road and then along the river-bank,' advised the groom. 'Careful. They're full of beans.'

Cuba shied violently at a piece of blowing paper, looked back to see if his rider was still there, saw that she was and gave in, trotting amicably onto the verge and turning to await his stablemate.

'How did you tame him?' asked Lin Chung. He was keeping his seat with ease and Phryne saw that he was a good rider; light hands and confident balance.

'I didn't tame him – he isn't tame. He's biding his time. Come on,' she saw a stretch of road, flat as a plate and grassy. 'Let's gallop.'

She dug her heels into Cuba's sides. He danced, complained, then put his head down and went like the wind. Lin galloped behind, admiring the grace of the flying horse and the rider, who had crouched down like a jockey, high on Cuba's shoulders. They looked like the pen painting he had seen in Shanghai of the mongol invaders; man and horse melded into one.

It was possible that Phryne never saw the obstacle. Cuba certainly didn't. In one moment, the sepia Ming drawing of fleeting horse and rider was destroyed. Cuba crashed to the road on his knees, and Phryne was flung over his head.

CHAPTER THREE

Great examples grow thin, and to be fetched away
from the passed world. Simplicity flies away, and
iniquity comes at long strides towards us.

Epistle Dedicatory, *Urn Burial*, Sir Thomas Browne.

LIN CHUNG leapt down and ran past the foun-
dered horse to where Phryne must have fallen. He
shoved aside the dense matted ti-tree, found a
gloved hand and then a shoulder, and hauled.

He gathered Phryne into his arms, feeling her
over for broken bones. Both collarbones intact,
and both legs and arms. He was stroking her hair
away from her face, checking for fractures, when
she sat up and said crossly, 'What in Hell's name
happened?'

'Cuba fell,' said Lin Chung. 'I thought you had
been killed – you should have been – you fall like
a cat, Silver Lady, like an acrobat. Where does it
hurt?'

'Everywhere,' she groaned. 'The secret of my

miraculous survival is ti-tree. Great stuff. Help me up, Lin, and we'll see to this poor hack.'

With Lin's arm around her, she limped back to Cuba, who was struggling to get up, nuzzled anxiously by the brown mare. Phryne called gently to the horse and he managed to regain his feet. Both his knees were bleeding.

'Poor Cuba. What on earth made you fall?' she took up each hoof in turn but there were no stones. Mopping at the horse's knees with her handkerchief she stared at the wound, silent for a moment. Then she gave the reins into Lin Chung's hand and said tautly, 'Tie them to a fence and come and look at this. This isn't a graze – it's a cut.'

Lin Chung looped the reins around a handy branch and did as requested. Cuba looked at him mournfully and he stroked his nose.

'Surely caused by the fall?' Lin Chung commented.

'He fell on grass, soft – well, relatively soft, grass. Walk back with me – ouch! God, I hit the ground hard. I saw bloody stars.' Lin supported her slight weight without trouble, feeling as anxious as the mare now licking at Cuba's knees.

'Look,' she said. A long thin tarred wire stretched from one side of the bridle-path to the other. It had been secured from fence to fence until Cuba's fall had broken it.

'More rustic humour?' asked Phryne, wincing as she straightened.

'Has it been there long?'

'No. The wire's new, not at all rusted, and it hasn't had time to bite into the wooden fencepost. What a nasty little mind – I wonder whose it is?' She coiled up the wire and stuffed it inside her shirt.

'You're shivering,' said Lin Chung, embracing her more closely. She laid her face against his warm chest for a moment, then remembered Cuba's legs, which would stiffen in the cold wind.

'I'm shocked. It's nothing. Bring the horses. We'd better get back.'

'The mare can carry you,' he said. Phryne was lifted without effort into the air and set down on the chestnut's back as lightly as a falling leaf. She kept her seat by instinct as Lin Chung led the horses back to Cave House.

The stableman rushed to meet them, wailing, 'I told yer 'e was frisky, Miss! Now look at 'is knees! Boss'll go crook, I tell yer that fer free.'

'I'll tell you another thing for free,' snapped Phryne, allowing Lin Chung to lift her down. 'You've got someone playing tricks. Have you seen anyone out along the bridle path today – or yesterday?'

'Why?' The gnarled brown face wrinkled with suspicion.

Phryne leaned on Lin and drew the coiled wire out of her shirt. The stableman squinted at it.

'Have you seen a snare like that before?'

'Yair. Dingo 'Arry uses that tarred wire for 'is dog traps. What of it?'

'That's what caused Cuba to come down like a ton of bricks and fling me over his head. If I hadn't been a fairly experienced rider I would have hit the road and been prematurely deceased. Now, be a nice man and stop snarling at me. I've had an exciting morning. I've got to sit down.'

The stableman, belatedly recognising that the rider was almost as battered as the horse, fetched her his own rush-seated chair and Phryne sagged into it.

'Ooh, my bruises are all settling down and raising families. Before I go and sink into a hot bath, composed mostly of arnica, I want a few answers. Your name?'

The small man dragged a handful of straw out of his hair and looked at her. This was the toff that the Mistress had been creating about for days, the Hon. from an aristocratic family in England. The one who had brought the Chow with her and caused a scandal. He was not disposed to liking rich people. However, she had controlled Cuba well and it did not seem to be her fault that he was now in need of Stockholm Tar and compresses.

'Me name's Terence Willis. They call me Terry. You're Miss Fisher, ain't you? Done a bit of ridin', I see.'

'A bit. You used to be a jockey, eh, Mr Willis?'

'How'd yer know that?'

Phryne smiled. He was small, light and bow-legged, with the curiously young-old face of a typical jockey. His hands, deformed from tugging on reins, were caressing Cuba passionately as the horse leaned its head on his shoulder and breathed down his shirt.

'There is nothing else you could have been, believe me. Someone laid a snare for the first rider along that track. Who would that normally have been?'

'Why, Mr Reynolds. He takes Cuba out every mornin' around dawn, 'cept today 'cos 'e slept in. 'E was up late.'

'Interesting. You say this Dingo Harry uses tarred wire for his dog-snares?'

'Yair, but he's all right, the ol' Dingo. Bit loony, but a lot of the swaggies are, comes of bein' on their Pat Malone so much. 'Arry's not the only bloke to 'ave a bit of tarred wire round the place. We got some 'ere, somewhere.'

'Indeed. Does Dingo Harry dislike Mr Reynolds?'

'Had a bit of a barney with the Boss about trespassin' – Dingo goes where 'e likes, 'e don't reckernize fences – 'e reckons all property is theft, anyway. Boss went crook and Dingo went crook and that was the end of it, far as I know.'

'Did you happen to see Dingo Harry on the bridle path in the last couple of days?'

'Nah,' the face screwed up again. 'But I ain't got all day to be loafin' about lookin' at the bridle path. Joe!' he yelled and a boy came running. 'Wrap a loose bandage round Cuba's knees and keep walkin' him up and down. I'll be there in a sec. You gonna tell the Boss about this?'

'Someone has to,' said Phryne, levering herself to her feet and leaning on Lin's ready arm.

Terry Willis adopted the expression of a small nut-brown gnome who has just watched his favourite toadstool being trodden on, hesitated, then said, 'Miss ... let's not be 'asty. The old Dingo, he's sorta a mate of mine, and ...'

'All right. Let's not leap to conclusions, either. You find Mr Dingo and see if he set this trap and warn him off if he did. But if it wasn't him, then I want you to come and tell me. Right away. Promise?' Willis nodded. Phryne continued, 'And it might be an idea if you take a pair of handy boltcutters and ride the bridle path yourself, every morning – just in case. Well, my bath calls. There's not much harm done, except to my pride – I haven't been thrown since I was thirteen.'

The old face creased into a thousand-wrinkle grin. 'Ah, Miss, if you'd been thrown as often as I 'ave, you wouldn't take it personal.'

Phryne laughed and left the stable.

'I know you could carry me,' she said to the hovering Lin Chung. 'But I don't need to make such a dramatic entrance. If I keep moving, like Cuba, I won't stiffen.'

'Why have you allowed that man to keep such a secret?' worried Lin. 'Shouldn't you tell Mr Reynolds that his life is in danger?'

'I think he knows, Lin dear. I think he already knows.'

Phryne had disrobed and soaked in a very hot bath, and was lying on her bed being anointed with goanna oil by a worried Dot when Mrs Reynolds knocked and was admitted.

'Phryne, you've been thrown! Terry Willis told me that Cuba threw you. Are you all right?'

'Just a few bruises. I landed rather awkwardly,' said Phryne, pleased that one part of the statement was true.

'I knew that horse was unsafe – I don't know what Tom was thinking of, buying a retired racehorse. I will have the creature shot.'

'Sit down, Evelyn,' requested Phryne, who was getting a crick in her neck trying to look up into her hostess's face. She could not allow Cuba to be executed. 'It wasn't the horse. Someone set a snare. A tarred wire across the road, just at knee height for poor Cuba. Evelyn, you wouldn't like to let me know what is going on, would you? I am a private investigator by profession.'

'I thought it was the horse,' said Evelyn. 'Willis told me that you were an all-right rider – that's a great compliment from him. Oh, God, and Tom rides every morning, along that bridle path. It was just pure luck that he didn't ride today, being up so late last night. It should have been him, and he wouldn't have just got a few bruises, would he?'

'No, he might have broken his neck,' said Phryne brutally. She allowed Dot to drape her in a loose gown and reclined on her pillows. 'Thanks, Dot, that feels divine. Slip down and get me a half bot of champagne, will you? I need a pick-me-up. Now, Evelyn, what is going on? I hear a shotgun blast in the mist, I rescue a parlourmaid who is scared out of whatever wits she had originally, and the next morning someone tries to kill me – or rather, Tom. When informed, Tom makes a joke of the whole thing and declines to take any of it seriously. Your maid was nearly raped and your husband was nearly killed – are you going to tell me about it?'

Mrs Reynolds flinched at Phryne's plain speaking. 'Oh, Phryne – ' she began, then stopped Dot at the door. 'Could you tell Hinchcliff to make it a full bottle of champagne. And two glasses.'

'Veuve Cliquot, if there's any in the cellar,' added Phryne. 'Come along, Evelyn, tell me all.'

'I . . . don't know where to start. I married Tom when we were both of a good age. I had been married before, I was a widow. I . . . had no children.'

Phryne noted the hesitation and said nothing.

'My family came out from home about one hundred and fifty years ago. They were squatters. We own a lot of land around here, even the grounds of Cave House used to belong to my grandfather. But we fell on hard times, you see, and there were only daughters in my family, no sons to carry on the name.' There Mrs Reynolds stuck.

Phryne said softly, hoping that Dot would arrive with the champagne soon, 'I do understand, you know. Until a lot of young men were killed in the War, I was living in desperate poverty. The Fisher fortunes were only rescued by marrying money – luckily Grandfather did.'

'Yes. That's what I did. I married a man much older than me, a manufacturer. Shoes. He lived in the city during the week but came home on weekends – and I did my part, I kept his house just as he wanted it. He paid off all the loans and mortgages, and when he died I married Tom. I married the first time out of familial duty. I married the second time out of love. Can you understand that?'

'Certainly,' murmured Phryne, shifting on her pillows and trying to find an unbruised hip to lean on.

'We came to live here most of the year. We don't like the city. After the War, things seem to have gone downhill – no one cares anymore for honour or stability or Empire. The music is discordant and the dancing is all ugly acrobatics. Yet manners are the only thing that keep us from anarchy. So I try to keep up propriety, you see, and order and precedence and dignity. Those things matter to me, matter very much.'

'How you must dislike having a raffish guest like me foisted on you – and bringing an unacceptable lover, as well!' mused Phryne. Mrs Reynolds flushed.

'Perhaps, at first, but your Mr Lin is so civilised, so polished, really, you wouldn't know he was Chinese at all!'

'Indeed,' said Phryne dryly. Dot entered with the Butler, who was carrying a silver tray on which reposed a bottle of Moët, two glasses in the highest state of polish, and a plate of dry salted biscuits.

Phryne was impressed. Far from being embarrassed at being in a bedroom with a lady in a state of undress, he was self-assured and dignified. He removed the foil and the wire basket, pulled out the cork with never a pop, and poured the sparkling wine with immense aplomb. He was a tall, stout man, with a magnificent corporation beneath his golden watchchain, and his linen was so white that it was giving Phryne eyestrain. His hair was grey and his hands, as they offered the tray, perfectly steady.

Phryne sipped. A good wine, though not the best. The butler put down the tray and left. Dot shut the door.

Mrs Reynolds gulped her wine with scant respect and Dot poured her another glass. There was a silence which stretched and thinned and Phryne did not break it.

'There have been letters,' said Evelyn, approaching the point at last.

'Letters? To Tom?'

'Yes. Five. I have them here.'

Phryne sat up too quickly, suppressed an oath, and scanned the papers.

'Have a look, Dot. See what you make of them. Written in blue pencil, no, indelible pencil, in printer's capitals. Are they in order of receipt? This is the first, then. YOU BARSTAD YOU CHEAT YOU SWINDLER YOU STOLE MY MONEY YOU LECHER YOU ... My, a fine flow of invective. Second letter, same words, different order. Third letter – aha! The threat. YOU BARSTAD YOU DISERV TO DIE and the

— 42 —

last, YOU BARSTAD ILE KILL YOU. Clear enough as to intention, sketchy as to execution.'

'This came yesterday,' said Mrs Reynolds, handing it over.

YOU DIE TODAY YOU SWINDLER, Phryne read. 'Same indelible pencil, same paper – what do you think, Dot?'

'Cheap,' said Dot critically, rubbing it between finger and thumb. 'But not real cheap. Not Woolworth's. No lines and foolscap size. I reckon it's typewriter paper, Miss. Same with the envelopes. Offices use long envelopes like that.'

'Thank you, Watson, what would I do without you? Go on, Evelyn. Now, you have a suspect, don't you?'

'Yes, so to speak, but I . . . can't believe it of him.'

'Who? Dingo Harry?' said Phryne, deliberately breaking her agreement with the stableman. This was more serious than it had first appeared.

Mrs Reynolds was taken aback. 'How on earth did you know about Dingo Harry?'

'I have my methods,' said Phryne, sipping Moët. 'You think he sent these missives?'

'He might have. He and Tom had a terrible fight about him slipping through our fences and snaring dingoes on our grounds. I don't know why it upset Tom so much but it did. He bellowed at Harry and Harry bellowed back and it almost came to blows.'

'Leaving aside the unlikelihood of a swaggie getting hold of typing paper, why should he call Tom a cheat and a swindler?'

'No reason. It's not Dingo Harry I'm thinking

of, though he seems most likely for the snare. In fact I wish it was Dingo Harry; he's a madman and they'd just lock him up for life. He doesn't matter. It's Jack, you see. Jack Lucas.' Evelyn wrung her hands.

'The tall blond boy? Why should he call Tom a cheat?'

'Jack Lucas's father and Tom were partners in a business. Tom got out before old Mr Lucas put all his money into the Megatherium Trust. It crashed and Lucas was ruined – went into a decline and finally put a bullet through his head. It was terrible, such a scandal, you must remember it. His wife died of grief and everything was sold up and poor Jack, who's been to a good school and educated to go to the university, has to get a job as an auction clerk and he's awfully unhappy about it. And the really terrible thing about it was that he asked Tom for a loan, to put him through university and pay his fees and so on, promising faithfully to pay him back, and Tom refused. He lost his temper, poor silly man, you know how men are. He said something about like father, like son, and that he wasn't a safe investment. Then Jack said that all Tom had done in his life was produce second-rate books and the only wisdom he'd shown was in marrying a rich wife. Oh, dear, there was a dreadful row and it took me days to talk them around. But Tom still won't lend Jack the money.'

'Can't you?' asked Phryne. 'It's your money, after all.'

Mrs Reynolds was so shocked that Dot had to pour her another glass of Moët.

'Miss Fisher ... all that I own is my husband's. I can't think of acting against his wishes,' she said as stiffly as three glasses of champagne in quick succession would allow. Phryne sighed.

'Of course, how silly of me. So. Jack Lucas might have written them. Yes. It's possible. The spelling is too good to be really illiterate. One would think that someone who doesn't know how to spell "bastard" or "deserve" would not know how to spell "swindler" or "money". However, what use is Tom dead to Jack Lucas?'

'Tom's left Jack a thousand pounds in his will. He wants to make up for the loss, you know, but he feels terribly guilty and that makes him tetchy. What's more Jack approached him the wrong way, asking for an advance on his inheritance, and Tom called him a beggar eager to wear dead men's shoes. Oh dear, oh dear, what am I to do?'

'The easiest thing to do is give Jack the money. If that doesn't suit, Tom should go to town and change his will and make sure that everyone knows that he's changed it. Then there'll be no reason to kill him.'

'Oh, no, he'll never do that. He won't go back on his word and he told old Lucas that he'd provide for his son.' Evelyn set down her glass unsteadily.

'Let him provide for the boy, then,' said Phryne in her most reasonable tone.

'Not after that dreadful quarrel.'

'Perhaps I could talk to him,' Phryne continued. Mrs Reynolds put out a hand to stop her as if fearing that her excitable guest was about to leap out of bed and beard the Master of the House in his den.

'Oh, no, he'd be terribly offended and hurt if he knew I was talking like this about him. He trusts me.'

'Evelyn, I've given you my advice. It's up to you to persuade Tom to take it. By the way, is there anyone else who has a grudge against Tom?'

'No, not that I know of. Of course, that Fletcher woman tried very hard to snare him when he lived in town, but she's now occupied with throwing poor Judy at Gerry Randall. I can't imagine why she wants him, she's as rich as Croesus already. The girl is a great catch, though I suppose that you can't really be too rich. And I've often wondered why Tom invites Major Luttrell here, he doesn't seem to like him much. But gentlemen will have their fancies, won't they?'

'They will,' agreed Phryne. Her current fancy was lodged far too far away from her with only his Confucianist principles to keep him warm. Mrs Reynolds rose.

'I really should go – Doctor Franklin is attending Lina and I really should be there.'

'Yes. See if you can find out what she isn't telling. She must have seen something if the man was close enough to ...' Phryne censored her words in deference to her hostess's sensibilities, 'assault her. And what was she doing out of the house, anyway? Surely your housekeeper doesn't encourage the maids to wander.'

'Certainly not. Mrs Hinchcliff is very strict. Even if she were not, Lina is her niece. Miss Fisher, thank you for listening to me. I must go,' she said, drawing herself up to her full height and smoothing down her tweed costume. Dot let her out.

'The old school trained its daughters well, Dot. There aren't many of them left in these parlous days. Thank God,' said Phryne, and drained her glass.

Phryne was recovered enough to come down to lunch. She endured some mild teasing from Gerald, Jack and Judy about her horsemanship, flirted mildly with the poet and Gerald and drank a little consommé.

The poet was gallant in a middle-European way. He raised his glass of hock in a toast.

'To Miss Fisher – most beautiful of Dianas.'

'I suppose even Diana took the occasional toss,' giggled Judy to Gerald, who smiled, and to Jack who did not.

'Beware lest you suffer the fate of Actaeon,' warned Tom, which silenced Judy.

Gerald caught on instantly. 'I'll try not to surprise you bathing, Miss Fisher.'

'I'm not likely to be in the position – far too cold for swimming.'

'Letty,' said the Major in a poisonous whisper heard perfectly by everyone at the table. 'Stop that blubbering and sit up straight.'

Mrs Luttrell whimpered, bit her lip, and took up a spoonful of soup. Phryne was trying to be sorry for this obviously oppressed woman but couldn't quite manage it. She had married the repellent Major, so she should find some way of dealing with him. Braining him with a handy chafing dish was Phryne's current favourite.

'So, you don't go for an early morning dip, Miss Fisher?' bellowed Major Luttrell. 'Should try it. Tones you up. The young chaps always do. I've seen 'em with their towels and togs running down to the jolly old river at the crack of dawn.'

'I'm toned enough, thank you,' said Phryne firmly.

Miss Mead remarked, 'I do think that the amount of physical exercise that gels do now must have something to do with their dress. So sensible! Flying planes and driving cars and climbing mountains, so difficult in long skirts and ... er ... garments.'

Before Judith could embarrass Miss Mead by asking her about her corsets, as Phryne could see she was preparing to do, she put in, 'Yes, Miss May Cunliffe won the London-to-Cairo road race, and women currently hold a number of records in aviation. Are you interested in planes, Miss Fletcher?'

'Of course not,' snapped her mother. 'Most unbecoming.'

Judith, who had been about to reply, shut her mouth and turned a trying shade of brick-red. Gerald said hastily, 'Do you fly, Miss Fisher?'

'Certainly,' said Phryne. 'Look me up when you're in town and I'll take you for a spin.'

The young man lowered lavish eyelashes and murmured, 'Oh, thanks, that would be lovely.'

Phryne was susceptible to lavish eyelashes and modesty. She smiled on the young man. Lin Chung, declining to play the game, was nevertheless paying close attention to the conversation. Phryne hoped that his principles were taking a battering.

'Did you go to school in China, Mr Lin?' asked Judith, too loudly.

'Oxford, actually,' he drawled. 'I have been to China, of course. But I was born in England.'

'Really?' Judith was again on the verge of saying something unwise but Phryne was devoid of conversational gambits. The discourse at the table was as forced as the early woody peaches which the poet was peeling with a silver knife.

'What do you do, Mr Lin? Are you a mission worker?'

'No, I am a silk importer,' he replied politely. 'Silk to make gowns for beautiful ladies.'

'Ah, silk,' rhapsodised the poet. 'Whenas in silks my Julia goes . . .'

Mrs Reynolds obviously knew the rest of the poem and considered it indelicate, or at least unfit for the luncheon table. She rose in her place to mark the conclusion of the meal and the guests straggled out. Lin Chung was claimed by Judith, who grabbed him by the hand, insisting on tennis, and Phryne accompanied Gerald and Jack out through the french windows and on to the porch.

'Do you care for a walk, Miss Fisher?' asked Gerald.

Phryne saw Lin Chung dragged away by Judith and smiled ironically. 'Certainly,' she said, tucking a hand under each elbow, 'but only to the rose garden. I'm still sore from that fall.'

'Just to the rose garden,' agreed Jack.

CHAPTER FOUR

The treasures of time lie high, in urns, coins and
monuments, scarcely beneath the roots of some
vegetables.

Urn Burial, Sir Thomas Browne, Chapter I.

THE ROSE garden already contained Miss Mead
and Miss Cray, so Phryne and her companions
kept walking. The original conceit of the builder
of Cave House had stretched to a knot garden
which might have been laid out by William Morris
himself. It was wet and scented and Phryne sniffed
with pleasure as she sat down on a Pre-Raphaelite
box bench which could have supported a medieval
King, with room left over for the rest of the court.

'Here's rosemary, that's for remembrance,'
quoted Gerald, laying a snippet of it in her lap. 'I
pray you, love, remember.'

'I'll remember,' said Phryne. He knelt beside her,
his brown eyes like a spaniel's. He was very attractive in a dewy, fragile fashion. Phryne could not

imagine a more unfitting mate for him than that rough, maladroit girl.

'Beautiful Miss Fisher,' he said, 'I have a favour to ask.'

'Gerry, get up, don't be an ass,' said Jack violently.

'Go away, Jack,' said Gerald, never removing his gaze. 'Aren't you supposed to be escorting Miss Cynthia to Bairnsdale about now?'

Jack swore and kicked the bench. Then there was the sound of running feet as he retreated towards the house. Phryne ran a meditative hand through Gerald's silky, curly hair. She knew when she was being charmed, but that didn't make her dislike the process.

'Get up, precious, sit beside me,' she said. 'You'll plead just as well in that position and the damp will ruin your flannels.'

A little disconcerted, the young man did as ordered and repossessed himself of Phryne's hand. 'You see, you're one of Mr Reynolds' oldest friends, he might listen to you. It's about Jack. He's my dearest chum, boyhood companion and all that. Tom Reynolds did his father out of a lot of money and won't give him a bean.'

Phryne cut him short. 'I know all about it, Gerald, and I'll try. But it may not work. And in return . . .'

'In return?' The spaniel-brown eyes loomed closer.

'You can help me in my investigation,' she said, and kissed him, decisively, on the mouth.

He tasted sweet, of early strawberries, perhaps. He kissed beautifully. Phryne finally dragged herself away and stroked one finger lightly along his cheek, which was flushed with the most delicate rose.

'Tell me about Jack, and Dingo Harry, and everything about Cave House,' she said.

'I'll show you around, may I?' he asked eagerly.

Phryne was feeling her injuries and was, besides, flooded with lust, an emotion which could not properly be transferred to such slender shoulders as Gerald's, who might snap under the strain. She hoped that Lin Chung was enduring a really punitive game of tennis and turned to accompany Gerald back to Cave House.

'Phryne,' someone called. 'Phryne, dear, there you are.'

'Here I am,' she agreed. 'Hello, Tom.'

'Been looking for you, old girl. Haven't shown you my house. Sorry, Gerry,' he said to the young man. 'Got to cut you out. Prior acquaintance and all that.'

Phryne gave Gerald a combustible smile and said, 'Another time.'

Gerald faded away in the direction of the stables and Phryne looked at Tom Reynolds.

His clipped speech was not unusual. She put it down to the years of sub-editing he had been forced to do before he left newspapers and took to books. He still spoke in headlines. He took her arm and returned the inspection; a stout, red-faced and jolly man, now looking strained and tired. His scanty grey hair was rumpled and Phryne smoothed it down across his pink scalp with an affectionate caress. He always reminded her of a teddy bear.

'Amazing house, Tom dear,' she commented with perfect truth. 'I've never seen anything like it.'

'Yes, it's a bit of a mishmash, but the brewer who built it, old Mr Giles, built well. It's got foundations down to the middle of the world and it's all good material – mahogany and cedar and fine cut stone. Of course, he'd made several fortunes – always safe putting your money into beer. Odd cuss. You were sitting on his tomb.'

'I was?' asked Phryne, rather startled.

'Yes, he planted several of his relatives around here. He's in the knot garden, his wife is in the rose garden, under a lot of *Mademoiselle Bichot* teas, and the house is full of urns of his nearest and dearest. He sold the place to Evelyn's father on the understanding that we take care of the urns, so we have. There's a marble one on your mantelpiece, I think.'

'Lord, Tom, you might have warned me! I thought it was a tobacco jar!'

'Lucky you don't smoke a pipe,' he chuckled. 'I was all for banishing them to the cellar but m'wife didn't think that was right, and I've got used to them. How did you get on with Evelyn?'

'Very well. She came to see me after I fell off Cuba.'

'He's a touchy one. Are you all right, Phryne?

Not like you to be thrown. Well, let's have a look at the house.'

'Tom, there's something very wrong here,' she said soberly as she limped across the lawn.

'What, with the house?' He laughed uncomfortably.

'Pay attention, Tom. Look, you know me. You should know that you can trust me. You've been ignoring or playing down two nasty happenings lately. Now that suggests to my suspicious mind that you are either fully aware of the situation and want to deny it, or that you are constitutionally obtuse, and I've never known you to be obtuse, Tom. You're in trouble.'

The bright brown eyes blinked at her unladylike frankness. He began, 'Now, Phryne, old fellow . . .' then sank under her cool green gaze. 'Oh, well, what's the use. You will have picked up all the gossip anyway by now, you're such a sponge for atmosphere. Yes, there is something happening. I've had letters. Someone wants to kill me. It's been going on for a while and I'm sick of it – but there's nothing I could go to the police with, Phryne, just insinuations. I heard about the tarred wire that brought poor Cuba down and could have killed you. That must have been aimed at me. Oh, God, here's Joan Fletcher.'

'Tom,' said Mrs Fletcher, pink with indignation, 'my daughter . . .'

'Your daughter?' asked Tom tonelessly.

'She's playing tennis with that Chinese person.'

'Yes?'

— 55 —

Mrs Fletcher drew in a deep breath and said in a voice loaded with horror, 'And she's laughing!'

'Joan, perhaps you might like to come back into the house and have some tea, you're overwrought,' said Reynolds. Joan Fletcher accepted his arm, almost pushing Phryne aside. Mrs Fletcher was dressed in trailing mauve chiffon, a most unsuitable garment for walking in but a becoming colour for her pale complexion and grey eyes. She leaned languishingly on Tom, and Phryne wished that she had kept hold of Gerald. If anyone was going to lean languishingly on a suitable man she wished it to be herself.

'Listen!' Joan said compellingly. Tom and Phryne listened.

From the roof came the sounds of a tennis ball hit fairly and hard, back and forth – *pock*, *pock*, *pock*. The rally went on for more than a minute. Then they heard *puck*! as the ball hit the wall behind and Miss Fletcher said, 'Well played!' and laughed.

Her mother was right. It was a light, genuine laugh and Phryne for one had never heard the girl laugh like that before.

'You're imagining things,' said Tom, pulling his eyebrows down out of his hair and shooting Phryne a questioning glance. Phryne shrugged. With his high ideas on reputation and female virtue, Lin Chung was no threat to Miss Fletcher's virgin state, but she could not see a way of telling Tom that without outraging Mrs Fletcher.

'I'm sure it will be all right,' she said. They stood

for a while, listening as the tennis players finished their game. Feet rang on the stairs.

Miss Cray and Miss Mead joined them on the portico.

'How nice to see the young people enjoying themselves,' murmured Miss Mead. 'I am not an expert, of course, but Mr Lin seems to be a very good tennis player. So graceful! I have been sitting up there watching them.'

Phryne thought that she detected a note of irony in the soft, well-bred voice, but could not be sure. So Miss Fletcher and Lin Chung had been provided with a chaperone. Mrs Fletcher sagged a little with what might have been relief. Equally, Phryne sensed an unwholesome excitement under the mauve chiffon. Was Mrs Fletcher willing her daughter to make a scandal, perhaps, or – no, not as serious as that – to fall in love, tragically, and need a mother's helping hand and wise counsel, to share the excitement of a love affair? If so, she seemed doomed to disappointment. Judy came clattering down the stairs with Lin Chung behind her, flushed with nothing more sinful than exercise.

'I say, spiffing game,' she exclaimed. 'Play again, Mr Lin?'

'Certainly.' Phryne saw that Lin Chung was not even breathing hard, much less sweating, and his cream flannels were unmarked. She caught his eye and he smiled and made a dismissive gesture with one hand – a bagatelle, it seemed to say.

'Tea,' said Tom Reynolds, and ushered them into the parlour.

A small table contained a pot of tea and one of coffee, which Phryne decided to avoid, and a plate of homemade ginger biscuits. Mrs Reynolds, apparently quite recovered, dispensed cups and the company sat down.

They were joined by Gerald, who wafted in and leaned on the doorpost.

'Remarkable library,' he said. 'Tom dear, whoever gave you all those books? Have you read them?'

'Don't be puckish,' begged his host. 'Life is too short to watch young men being puckish, even decorative young men like you. Why, what have you found?'

'The *Yellow Book*,' said Gerald. 'You've got a complete collection with Beardsley illustrations. Surely old brewer Giles can't have bought such inflammable literature.'

'No, I believe that it was his wife,' said Tom. 'She had artistic pretensions. Now, do you want some tea or not?'

'Gerry, how about a nice game of tennis?' suggested Miss Fletcher. 'You don't want to frowst about in the rotten old library all day.'

'Yes I do,' he said sweetly. 'You've got a partner, Judy. Play with him, he's much better than me. I'm a real duffer at tennis. No tea, thanks, Mrs Reynolds.'

He wafted out again, and Judith declared to the company, 'I believe he's jealous!'

There was a dead silence. Lin Chung rescued the situation.

'You promised me another game, Miss Fletcher,' he said, putting down his untouched cup and picking up his racket.

Phryne gave him ten out of ten for gentlemanly behaviour.

'Such a nice day,' commented Miss Mead. 'Though it looks like rain, I fear.'

'Yes, and the river is rising. We shall be cut off if it comes up another foot. Nothing to worry about,' said Mrs Reynolds. 'We have a large store of food and the water never comes up beyond the knot garden or the stables. Just a matter of waiting it out. I hope that Jack and Cynthia will be all right, though. Sometimes the river cuts the road.'

Phryne spared a few enjoyable moments wondering what Jack Lucas would do with the voluptuous and predatory Miss Medenham if they were cut off by floodwater, decided that he would be equal to the challenge, and drank her tea. Miss Cray who had ostentatiously refused sugar said, 'I never take sugar. I gave up during Lent some years ago. Austerity is my goal.'

'Very fitting,' murmured Miss Mead, getting out her crocheting.

'Very,' agreed her host. 'It does you credit, Sapphira.'

'How is that poor parlourmaid?' asked Miss Mead of Miss Cray. 'You were going to visit her.'

'Yes, but that Doctor would not let me in. I left her a few tracts. At such times one must think of one's soul.'

'Indeed,' agreed Miss Mead. 'It was strange that

she was attacked so far from the house. Still, I expect that it was a wandering madman, some tramp – poor girl. Do you like this new pattern, Miss Cray? It's for my cousin's child and I am a little doubtful about the edging.' Miss Cray unbent enough to give an opinion on the delicate shell pattern. Mrs Fletcher joined in with reminiscences of Brussels and the lace she had bought there for Judith's baby frocks, and Phryne drifted to Tom Reynolds' side.

'Come on, old thing, let's escape,' she murmured, and he put down his cup. They were just approaching the door when the Doctor came in.

Doctor Franklin was a tall, slim man, with fashionably pale skin and slightly long dark hair, brushed straight back from a high forehead. His eyes were of an indeterminate shade between grey and blue and his profile was pure matinee idol; high-nosed, Roman and refined. He gave Phryne a smooth, well-tended hand and said, 'Ah, Miss Fisher, how delightful to meet you. How do you do?'

'Very well, thank you.'

Now that she could see him close up, he was not as young as he looked, or as confident. The hand had a slight but definite tremor; the palm was damp. There were fine lines around his eyes, extending into grooves around his finely chiselled mouth. She seemed to remember hearing that he had taken a leave of absence from his booming Collins Street practice with 'nervous exhaustion', a portmanteau term which could cover everything from the occasional headache to a full-blown hysterical collapse.

'Miss Cray, Miss Mead, good morning,' he said, looking past Phryne and releasing her hand. 'Yes, thank you, Mrs Reynolds, I would like some tea.'

Phryne and Tom escaped into the reception hall and Tom wiped his brow with a blue handkerchief.

'Phew! What a collection. Come along, I want to show you the house.'

'All right, Tom dear, but if you don't like your guests, why on earth do you invite them?'

'Reasons,' said Tom obscurely. He led the way through a green baize door into a dark little hall. He knocked on a closed door which was lettered 'Butler's Pantry' and called, 'Hinchcliff, I'm taking Miss Fisher on a tour. Can I have the cellar keys?'

Mr Hinchcliff, magnificent even though his waistcoat was unbuttoned and he had been evidently putting his boots up for a rest when his master called. He emerged and detached the keys from his watchchain.

'Don't forget the stairs are slippery, Sir,' he warned.

Phryne was conducted down the corridor and into the servants' hall, which contained the staff having morning tea. Dot was introducing Li Pen to ginger biscuits. Mrs Croft the cook was listening to his account, in his hesitant, accented English, of the home life of ginger. The rest of the staff were talking amongst themselves and the boy Albert was sitting on the back doorstep playing mumblety-peg with a jackknife. It whizzed past Phryne's ankle. The boy gaped, grabbed the knife, and fled into the yard a scant inch ahead of Tom's foot.

'Young devil,' said Tom indulgently.

'I'll tan his hide,' said Mrs Croft. 'Little monster! Mr Black, can you catch the little blighter?'

'No,' said the mechanic, glancing out the window. 'He's got a fair turn of speed, Mrs C – he'll be miles away by now.'

He went on with his tea.

Phryne surveyed the table. Mr Black, from the indelible grease, was evidently the chauffeur and machine-minder. He had extended his range of skills so far as the carving and setting of a pile of very neat wooden clothes pegs. Mr Jones, who was a deal cleaner, seemed to be the houseman. Mrs Croft, a formidable woman in an apron so starched that it bent around her ample figure, was Cook. An earthy person and attendant, even earthier, had to be the gardeners. A scruffy girl with a mass of chestnut hair escaping from its bonds and water-wrinkled hands, was obviously the scullery maid and kitchen dogsbody. She was staring into her cup as though expecting reproof on its cleanliness. Mrs Hinchcliff was not there – perhaps she was with the distressed maid Lina. Dot, sitting between Li Pen and Terry Willis, smiled at Phryne.

Li Pen had obviously graduated from 'Chink who might be Fu Manchu's advance agent', to 'Chink who was a nice bloke really and quite a pet and very well informed about ginger'. Phryne was glad to see it. The servants were adapting faster than the guests, which was, perhaps, to be expected. Li Pen accepted another biscuit and Dot refilled his cup.

'Just taking Miss Fisher on the grand tour,' apologised Reynolds. 'Didn't mean to disturb anyone.' For the place of the Boss was in the house and the place of the staff was in the servants' hall and the twain were not supposed to invade each other's domains.

Mrs Croft, as senior officer, inclined her head graciously as Phryne and Tom went on.

The cellar was reached by a Gothic stone stair which would not have disgraced a castle. It was, as the butler had said, slippery.

'There's a well down here,' said Tom. 'We dug another outside the house and capped this one, but it's dangerous in the dark.' He pulled on a cord and a bare electric bulb flicked into life. 'I've got my own generator. I can't be having with lamps, even though Evelyn says they cast a softer light. Too much work for the staff. I'd have to employ a boy just to clean and fill them and I already employ half the locals as it is. I'd better get Black and Jones down here with a pump. The river's rising.'

'Does it often flood?'

'Every seven years or so. Never been bad since I've been here – old Mr Giles was flooded in for weeks in the old days. Water never gets up to the house but the cellar is below the watertable so we get seepage.'

'I see you inherited Mr Giles's wines.' She looked at rows and rows of bottles marked with cellarman's whitewash.

'And I've been adding to them,' agreed Tom. 'There's good wine coming out of the Barossa now, some reds that I've laid down for ten years; good port and tokay, even a rather tasty light hock. Quite passable with soda.'

The cellar was very large. It seemed to run most of the length of the house above. In the dim, unlit recesses, Phryne could see a jumble of old furniture; broken sideboards and chairs, what could surely not have been a marble sarcophagus, a pile of obsolete chamber-pots, and a stack of mildewing chests.

'Junk,' said Tom. 'And there's more in the attic. Come on, it's cold.'

'About this threat to your life?'

Reynolds was about to speak, then shut his mouth. 'Not here. We can be overheard.' He pointed up to where the servants' hall probably was. The sound of tinkling spoons and crockery being collected could be heard. Li Pen was saying, 'Ginger is given to make a horse strong and fast,' and she heard Terry Willis chuckle. 'Yair, I've known it to happen, 'specially when it was put under its ...' he dried up with the concluding word 'tail' unsaid, probably under Mrs Croft's glare.

Tom Reynolds grinned and led the way up the castle staircase to another, which was by contrast lined with panelled wood and smelt of beeswax.

'This is the first floor,' he said to Phryne as she emerged behind him. 'Bedrooms and guestrooms and the like. I put in bathrooms and lavatories as soon as I realised that I was going to live here.' They walked along a passage heavy with plaster mouldings in the shape of cornucopias to another stair.

Phryne's knees were tiring and her bruises were all shouting at once. But the movement was unstiffening her and she picked up her pace to keep up with her host.

'Here are the servants' rooms and the attic.' Tom seemed determined to exhibit his whole house to Phryne. She opened a door at random and approved of a small room with an iron bed, a wardrobe, one window, a light, a smudgy picture of a child with an umbrella, and the ubiquitous servant's trunk, known as a box, on a stand.

'Very nice,' she said. 'Where to next?'

'The roof,' he said.

They skirted the dome, which dominated the hall, and Phryne looked down, leaning on a carved railing. The tea party was breaking up. She saw Miss Cray and the Doctor pass through the hall together, deep in discussion. Miss Mead and Mrs Fletcher were mounting the monumental stairs, talking about grades of wool and the need to keep babies warm. The staircase was lined with portraits of someone's ancestors, urns on brackets, and a huge oil painting of a fox-hunt, strong on horses, so aged and smoky that only the hunting pink of the riders was visible.

Gerald emerged for a moment from the library, keeping his place in a yellow-covered book. Then he brightened and ran across the marble tiles to the front door to greet Jack Lucas escorting an unmistakable Miss Medenham in a bright-red coat and hat.

'I say,' Phryne heard him say. 'I say, Gerry, isn't it exciting? The road's two feet deep in water. We're cut off.'

CHAPTER FIVE

If they died by violent hands ... whose souls they conceived most pure, which were thus snatch'd from their bodies, and to retain a stronger propension unto them. We live with death, and die not in a moment.

Urn Burial, Sir Thomas Browne, Chapter V.

For some reason, Phryne's heart sank.

Tom grunted and led the way, under the magnificent Pre-Raphaelite leadlight windows of medieval scenes, up yet another stair – this time decorated with frescos of dancing Greek maidens – to the roof.

Lin Chung and Judith Fletcher were playing tennis on the court which occupied half of the roof. The other half was paved and it was all edged with a low marble balustrade.

'Phryne,' groaned Tom. 'I'm for it now. I'm shut in with my murderer.'

'Don't be silly, Tom dear. I have no intention of

allowing you to be murdered; my reputation won't stand it.'

The prospect was very pleasant. A cool wet wind blew into Phryne's face. Far away she could see a craggy line of mountains, blue in the distance. Closer there was a ridge of yellowish hue, which Tom said was the Buchan Caves. A tributary of the Snowy River curved around Cave House; gun-metal water, running fast and creamy with foam. It was an uncomfortable neighbour.

They turned away from the sight and watched the tennis players in silence for a moment. Judith Fletcher was robust and reasonably agile; she puffed as she ran and lunged. Lin Chung, in his immaculate creams, moved like a cat, seeming to anticipate every lob, returning it with precise, effortless blows, calculated not to be impossible to reach but to give his partner a strenuous game. He was indulging Miss Fletcher, Phryne decided, which was nice of him.

'He's a gentleman.' Tom had reached the same conclusion.

'Of course he is. Now, are you going to let me help you or not?'

'Yes, yes.' He scrubbed at his forehead distractedly. 'Of course, that's why I asked you here, or one of the reasons, Phryne dear. Evelyn wanted to meet you. I owe all this to Evelyn. This was her house, her money.'

'Yes, I know that.'

'So I want to please her. This house party was her idea. I'd be perfectly happy to only ask just one or two people – you and Mr Lin for instance, people I like, like Tadeusz. But Evelyn was brought up in the old tradition, tennis parties, cricket parties. They don't seem to match Australia, Phryne dear, you can't get a biddable well-trained staff like you can in England. I mean, what would you do if you were offered a choice of working in the pickle factory, where you'd have money in your pocket and be your own mistress, or room and board and two and six a week out here in the bush with Mrs Hinchcliff watching your every move?'

'The pickle factory,' said Phryne promptly.

'Exactly. So I'm practically running an asylum. All the bold intelligent children go to the city. The weak and wambling go into service. I've got Lina who's a neurasthenic, Mrs Croft who has a fetish about cleanliness, Jones who's got a criminal record, Willis who's crippled, a housemaid with two illegitimate children and . . . you see? If I pro-claim we've got a murderer amongst us they'll all fall to bits so fast there will be shrapnel wounds. Even Mr and Mrs Hinchcliff are worried.'

Phryne patted his arm.

'So we do it very quietly. I can just drift around and pick up gossip and Dot can do the same, that covers both worlds. And you should pay some attention to your own safety, Tom. Don't be alone with Jack Lucas, try not to have arguments with Dingo Harry – I must meet him, he sounds most refreshing – and keep your head down. It might all be malicious mischief, not a real threat at all.

And for God's sake, either change your will or give Jack Lucas his money.'

Tom Reynolds stiffened but she went on relentlessly. 'I've never known you to be unjust, Tom dear. It's messy, leaving someone loose with such a good reason to kill you. If you fall off the house or something, the poor boy'll be arrested before you can say Jack Robinson. Do something about it, even if he has got right up your nose to an alarming extent. Now I want to talk to Lina.'

'She's still having the vapours,' objected Tom.

'And she is entitled to have any vapours that she wants. But I want to talk to her. Come along. Take me to her.'

The *pock, pock, pock* of the tennis game faded behind them as they went down the stairs.

Doctor Franklin was closing the door when they arrived. Paul Black walked past, smeared and unhurried, trailing a bundle of electric flex.

'She's asleep,' he said, in reply to Phryne's request. 'She'll be awake by tea time, then she should be able to talk to you, Miss Fisher. She's a nervous subject, however, and she's still greatly shocked by whatever it was that happened out there.'

The Major, passing on his way to the parlour, greeted Phryne and his host. 'Tom, Miss Fisher.' His eyes lingered on Phryne. 'How about a game of billiards, Tom? Do you play, Miss Fisher?'

'A little,' Phryne said, knowing that Tom Reynolds had honed his billiards-playing skill to shark levels as a journalist and hoping that he would skin the Major of his entire worldly wealth. 'Not up to your standard, Major, I'm sure. You'll excuse me. Tom, I might go and have a nap until tea myself. It's a sleepy day.'

Dot was catching up the hem of Phryne's broadcloth coat with tiny, skilled, invisible stitches when her mistress came in and let herself gently down onto her bed.

'Well, Dot, I've been all over Cave House and my aesthetic sensibilities may never recover. How are you getting on?'

'Very well, Miss. The food's good and the company's quite nice. That Mr Li knows a lot about the world. He's been through the South China Sea with Mr Lin. And he was with him in Oxford. Did you talk to Mr Reynolds?'

'Yes, after a fashion, but I don't know if he was listening. Well, I'm going to have a rest.' Phryne removed her outer garments and her shoes and lay down on her bed. Dot finished her seam, snapped the thread off, and hung the coat in the wardrobe.

'I might go out for a walk, Miss,' said Dot artlessly. 'If you don't need me.'

'Oh, yes? With whom?'

'Mr Li,' she replied, and Phryne suppressed a number of indiscreet warnings.

'Good. Have a nice time,' she said, yawning.

Phryne was asleep, snuggled into the eiderdown, when she heard the doorhandle turn. Without moving, she awoke fully. The person opened the door, letting in a streak of sunlight. It was still early, then. She had not slept long.

One footstep sounded on the wooden floor, then was muffled in the carpet. It was heavier than Dot's tread and sounded like a man.

Phryne waited, breathing like a sleeper and wishing she had not tucked her head into her pillow so that she might be able to see who it was.

Outside, she heard birds singing. The intruder took a deep breath.

Phryne moved fast, flinging herself sideways and rolling off the bed, then leapt up and grabbed. She hooked his feet out from under him without difficulty.

A slim, light body, putting up no resistance, was flung onto the bed with Phryne's knees on his chest. Someone grunted, 'Golly, Miss Fisher!' and she recognised the voice.

'Gerald, what are you doing, creeping into my room?' she asked, exasperated, removing her weight from his torso, so the young man could sit up. This he showed no inclination to do, remaining sprawled across Phryne's bed like an odalisque.

'You're strong,' he cooed, stroking her shoulder and down to the arm and wrist.

'Good thing too,' observed Phryne.

At this point the doorknob rattled as it was tried. Someone else was violating Miss Fisher's siesta. For some reason, which she could not have explained, Phryne was suddenly very unwilling to be found by whoever was at the door.

'Quick.' Phryne dragged the young man down behind her bed, smothering his exclamation of surprise with her palm. After a second, he lay passively in her embrace, catching some of her disquiet.

The door opened. A man came in. Phryne could not identify him in the half-dark. He stood still for a while, allowing his eyes to become accustomed to the gloom. Then he walked ten paces, saw that the bed was empty, turned and went out, shutting the door behind him.

Phryne snorted, Gerald sighed. He was lying back in her arms. She replaced herself on her bed and said, 'I wonder who that was? Did you recognise him, Gerald?'

'No. Just a shape and a movement. A man, though.'

'Yes. A man.' She was sure that it was not Lin Chung, who walked like a cat, but otherwise it could have been any male person in the house. 'Now, Gerald, you haven't answered my question. What are you doing here?'

'Well . . .' The feather-light fingers processed up her arm again and lingered in the hollow of her collarbone.

'Well indeed,' said Phryne, observing his flushed face, glistening eyes and the curly hair fallen back from a marble brow. 'But it was unwise. I do not like being woken abruptly.'

'No, you don't, do you?' said the young man,

leaning up on one elbow. 'Did your Chinese teach you to fight like that?'

'No, an apache in Paris taught me – among other people. Get up, Gerald.'

'But . . .' he protested. Phryne kissed him firmly.

'I think you're absolutely beautiful,' she told him, extending a hand to help him to his feet. 'But this is not the way to approach me, Gerald. I've spoken to Tom Reynolds about Jack Lucas's inheritance, although I don't know what good it will do.'

He leaned into her embrace, trembling with some emotion – lust, perhaps, or gratitude – and whispered, 'I'll do anything for you, Miss Fisher.'

'I'll remember,' said Phryne dryly, wondering why she was not seducing this absolutely decorative young man. She reflected that she was either acquiring ethics, which did not seem likely, or just had a preference for the delectable Lin Chung – if she could get him. 'Perhaps it is time to call me Phryne. Now off you go,' she said, and firmly pushed him to the door.

She opened it. There was no one in the corridor. Gerald clung and Phryne kissed him again. His mouth was soft and skilled. She melted briefly, then pushed him away.

'I'll see you at dinner, Gerald. And we shall see,' she promised, closing the door and leaning on it, feeling the rush of adrenalin ebb.

'I could just shove the back of this chair under the door and resume my nap,' she said aloud. 'But now I'm far too awake to go back to sleep, dammit.' She crossly resumed her garments and found her walking shoes.

Who had come into her room? And why?

'Oh, my darling,' said the voice in the library. 'Oh, my own dear.'

'Hush,' said the other voice.

Mouth met mouth, lips soft as silk, red as flowers, exploring, tasting. Hands intertwined and clung desperately.

'It's no good,' wailed the first voice. 'They'll never let me go – never.'

'Hush,' said the second voice tenderly. 'Hush, sweet love, we'll be free. There will be a way. I know there will. There must be.'

A golden head and a dark head were laid close together and they stared into each other's eyes.

'We love each other so much,' said the first voice. 'And there's no cure for it, is there?'

'My true love hath my heart and I have his,' quoted second voice. 'Hush, love, don't be so violent. There'll be a way. Now kiss me again and let me go. I'll see you at dinner?'

'At dinner,' mourned first voice. 'And after that?'

'Don't be so greedy,' said second voice indulgently. 'We're flooded in, remember? They can't part us yet.'

'I'll hope for forty days and forty nights. Perhaps we should start building an ark. I'd like that. Just you and me and a few animals on the wide, wide sea.'

Second voice laughed.

When Phryne came in a few moments later, the library seemed empty.

It was an impressive collection of books, she thought, observing the ranked shelves of leather-bound volumes. All the walls were lined with shelves. A big mahogany table, the legs carved with satyrs in an advanced state of excitement, was laden with newspapers and paperback novels for railway reading, including *Midnight of the Sheik*, *Passion's Bondslaves* and *Silken Fetters*. Phryne picked one up, amused. She knew the author, the impeccably respectable Miss Eunice Henderson whose mother had been murdered on the Ballarat train. The market for drivel, Eunice had informed her, was always under-supplied.

Phryne was dipping into the lush prose of *Midnight of the Sheik* and trying not to laugh when a woman appeared from a distant alcove and said, 'That's where I left it.'

'Sorry, Miss Medenham, is this yours?' asked Phryne, closing the book and holding it out.

'Yes, I'm halfway through and just got to the bit where her English gentleman comes out to plead with her to return. Have you read it?'

'Not that one,' said Phryne, concealing the fact that hell would freeze over before she wasted her eyesight on *Midnight of the Sheik*. 'But I always wondered what novelists read.'

'Oh, as to my art, Miss Fisher, that's another

thing. It bubbles up from inside me, from the deep wells of creativity,' said Miss Medenham. 'Sometimes I feel that I am in touch with the other side – with other great writers who long to be reincarnated.'

'Oh? Who?'

Miss Medenham settled down for a cosy gossip about herself, automatically leaning back to emphasise her unfashionable bosom and crossing her long, slim legs. She was wearing a red jersey dress under the red coat, and champagne-coloured silk stockings. Her fair hair was shoulder length and straight as a drink of water. 'Emily Brontë, of course. Didn't you notice the fire and passion of my last novel, the depth, the wind blowing through it?'

Phryne wondered whether to admit that she had stuck fast three pages into the dense prose of *Earth*, Miss Medenham's latest offering. She decided that there would be too many ructions about it if she did, meaning that she would subsequently be both forced to read it and endure an inquisition about it from the author to make sure that she had appreciated it properly. Than which she would rather be boiled in oil. Phryne also suppressed the opinion that the bandit-lover had been remarkably clean and well-educated for a Spanish peasant, resembling rather an Oxford gentleman with picturesque trappings. *Earth* had been a book which cried out to be left lying behind the sofa whence it had fallen from the reader's nerveless hand.

'Of course,' she lied. 'Are you working on something new?'

'I'm waiting for inspiration,' said Miss Medenham. 'Actually, I was also looking for Jack. I thought he came in here.'

'An inspiring young man,' commented Phryne dryly.

'Yes,' Miss Medenham smiled suddenly, a complicit gamine grin, and Phryne liked her better immediately. She might write dreadful books, but she had a suitable appreciation of young men.

'Would a poet do as well?' asked Tadeusz from another alcove. Phryne decided that the library had never been empty – it had multiple hiding places. She filed the fact for future reference.

Miss Medenham raised her china-blue eyes and gave the poet an assessing glance. She stood up, smoothing down the clinging dress over her curved body, her hand lingering on one hip. 'Yes, I think you might be just as inspiring,' she decided. Tadeusz held out his arm and Miss Medenham sidled close to him.

They left the library together. Phryne, wondering if anyone else was tucked into the recesses, toured the shelves. The brewer who built it had probably never read anything but a lading bill in his life. His wife, however, had purchased full sets of all the classics, as well as a row of yellow-covered sprightly French romances and bound volumes of *Punch* and *Country Life*. She examined *Punch* briefly – Mafeking appeared to have been relieved – and read a few heavily satirical lines about Boers. Shoving the volume back onto the shelves, she reflected that nothing dates like topical humour.

The next alcove contained all the books which Tom had published himself, in no particular order. Books on *Furniture-making for the Beginner* flanked volumes on the *Horrors of War*, and slim suede-clad poets clung to strong female writings about Higher Thought. Phryne saw a book by an author she liked but *The Mysterious Affair at Styles* was wedged in between a volume of Victorian sermons and a very solid tome on Sanitary Reform. She slid the sermons out and a slip of paper dropped to the polished parquet.

TONIGHT, it promised in bold black capitals. USUAL PLACE.

Phryne was about to replace it when she was struck with a thought, and sat down to examine the note. She had seen those capitals before, that printer's Greek E.

The writer of the anonymous letters threatening Tom Reynolds' life was in the house. Phryne replaced the note in the sermons of the Reverend Patterson – by his prose a great benefactor to the insomniac – and resigned herself to the loss of the murder mystery. She did not want the note-writer to know that anyone had been near his or her correspondence.

Phryne walked the rest of the library. It was bigger than it looked, an oval room with four recesses, deep enough to hide in, two of which were provided with French windows which gave on to the portico. Perfect for conspirators; might have been designed for spies. Easy access from the rose garden on one side and the hall on the other.

Phryne was annoyed, worried and wishing she had some support. It might have been possible to keep a discreet watch on the alcove where the message had been left, but it would need three people at least. She did not want to involve Dot, she did not trust anyone else, and there was a coolness with Lin Chung which would naturally extend to his servant Li Pen.

Phryne swore and dismissed the matter from her mind. There was nothing much she could do about it at the moment. Now, which author would be reliable in a country house cut off from the outside world? Finally she found Sir Thomas Browne's *Hydriotaphia* and Dickens' *Bleak House*. Dickens was an author to travel with, and she had left her copy at home. She needed to occupy a couple of hours until she could talk to Lina.

She took her books into the drawing room, where Evelyn was consulting with Cook. Phryne sat down at the small table near the window and opened Sir Thomas. He always amused her. Such a precise and terribly learned man.

Hydriotaphia, urne buriall, or a difcourse of the sepulchrall urnes lately found in Norfolk, 1658, she read.

'Very well, Mrs Croft, we shall have egg and bacon pie, the veal chops, crumbed, I think, and the fish, of course, if the gentlemen catch any. I saw my husband and the Major going out with rods – they must have decided against the billiard room. It's such a nice day.'

'Yes, Madam,' said the cook, folding her hands

in her lap. 'Perhaps we ought to do a fricassee, in case they don't catch anything? The river's running a banker, Willis says, and Albert brought in some nice rabbits.'

'If you have time. Creamed potatoes, and have we any peas left?'

'Only tinned, Madam.'

'Tinned it will have to be. We're cut off from Bairnsdale at present, Mrs Croft. How are the supplies?'

'Well, we've got a cellarful of potatoes and onions, and a side of beef hanging. There's also those partridges and any amount of chooks and eggs, and we could send to Buchan Farm for butter and that soft cheese. I reckon we can hold out for a few weeks if we have to.'

'Good. What about dessert?'

When the funeral pyre was out, and the laft valediction over, men took a lafting adieu of their interred frendes, little expecting that the curiofity of future ages should comment upon their afhes, read Phryne, trying to block out the conversation.

'Apple pie, Madam, and cheese, and we've got some peaches in the greenhouse, for all that the gardener says they're too early. Otherwise we can have bottled apricots.'

But who knowes the fate of his bones, or how often he is to be buried? Who hath the oracle of his afhes, or whether they are to be fcattered? The relicks of many lie like the ruines of Pompeys in all partes of the earth; and when they arrive at your handes, these may seem to have wandered farre, who in a direct and median travel, have but few miles of known earth between yourfelf and the pole.

'Bottled apricots and cream,' decided Mrs Reynolds.

Phryne took Sir Thomas into the parlour.

When, at three-thirty, she went to the maid's door and knocked, there was no reply. The door was open. Phryne looked in and what she saw caused her to drop a valuable early copy of *Urne Buriall* to the floor with a thud which might have broken the spine.

Lina was not going to be able to tell her who had attacked her in the fog. A swollen countenance, blue with suffocation, confronted Phryne's horrified gaze. Black bruises showed on the throat.

Lina was dead.

CHAPTER SIX

The certainty of death is attended with uncertainties,
in time, manner and places.

Urn Burial, Sir Thomas Browne, Chapter III.

Phryne picked up the book, stepped back and
closed the door. Then she walked quickly to the
drawing room, passing Mrs Croft on her way back
to the kitchen.

It took some time to locate the Mistress of the
House. Phryne finally ran her down in the kitchen
garden, consulting with a grubby gardener's boy
about, it seemed, carrots.

'Evelyn, I have something to show you,' said
Phryne. 'Could you come with me, please?'

'Now, Phryne?' Mrs Reynolds looked up from
surveying a collection of muddy objects which
might, or might not, be vegetables.

'Yes, now, Evelyn,' she replied. Something in her
voice made Mrs Reynolds abandon her discussion
and follow Phryne obediently to Lina's room.

Phryne opened the door.

The bed was made up with clean sheets, drawn close and flat. The blue blanket and eiderdown lay innocent of one wrinkle. The window was open, the curtain flapped.

Of the dead woman there was not a trace.

'Where's Lina?' asked Mrs Reynolds.

'Where indeed?' asked Phryne, profoundly shocked. 'Is this the right room?'

'Why, yes, her name's on the door,' said Mrs Reynolds, pointing out the luggage label with a handwritten 'Lina' on it. 'Where can they have put her? Perhaps Mrs Hinchcliff has moved her to their suite, it's further along. Let's see, next door is the housemaid, then the scullery maid ...' She opened each door as she passed and Phryne looked in. Each room had the same bed and chair, the same box, and various rather dim or messy oils on the wall facing the window. Servants' rooms tended to be the destination of pictures and furniture that no one had the heart to throw out but didn't want to exhibit in any public rooms. Dot's powdering closet had a large gilt-framed painting of a few vague figures walking through a field which Phryne's companion had instantly disliked. Phryne had swapped her for *Hope*, which Dot thought well drawn.

The Hinchcliffs' suite was larger and well furnished in the standard Cave House melange of styles. It contained a tester-bed, a Turkish carpet, some mock-Sheridan chairs and a Gothic-revival table, a painting of three horses and a multitude of photographs in silver frames. In several of them, a younger Mr and Mrs Hinchcliff stared out, clutching a baby notable for its utterly blank expression. What it did not contain was Lina.

'I'd better talk to Mrs Hinchcliff,' worried Mrs Reynolds. 'She must have ordered Lina moved. Thank you for telling me, Phryne. I can't have my household shifted about like this.'

'Not at all,' said Phryne through lips which were as numb as novocaine.

In another three minutes she had found Lin Chung.

He was sitting in a leather armchair in the small parlour, reading her copy of *Bleak House*. She paused at the door and looked at him. The weak sunlight gilded his bent head and the long fingers turning the pages. He seemed as self-contained and decorative as a cat.

He felt her presence, lifted his head to speak and saw her expression. Her face was blanched and she looked like an ivory carving of some Buddhist deity. His urbane comment on Dickens' style died on his lips. He did not exclaim, but she saw hunting alertness sweep through him, so that even sitting in exactly the same pose, he was no longer relaxed but nerved for action. She walked deliberately forward and held out her hand.

'Come,' she said, and Lin Chung followed unquestioningly out of the house and across the lawn until she stopped under the beech tree. She led him around the trunk and then scanned the branches narrowly. In all that time she had not spoken and the hand in his was shaking. Then she slid both arms around his waist and held him tight as she began to speak. His arms closed around her.

'The body was gone?' he asked, five minutes later. 'I see. It is perfectly insane, but this is a good setting for the surrealist. Phryne, how dreadful. You are having a difficult day.'

This deliberate understatement produced a laugh, which pleased him. He sat down on the dry grass under the tree and gathered Phryne into his embrace. She tucked her head under his chin. He admired her immensely. She was still trembling with shock but she was reasoning like a sage.

'She was dead,' she said firmly. 'Strangled. How hard is it to strangle someone, Lin?'

'Easy,' he said. 'With sufficient strength of heart.'

'Show me,' she requested.

Reluctantly, Lin Chung laid both hands to her slim throat, thumbs at the front. He pressed lightly. 'You see, here is the pressure point. And here is the great blood vessel that supplies the brain. All I need to do is grip hard enough to cut off that blood supply, and you would be unconscious in – well, maybe a minute – and . . .' He stopped.

'Dead in five minutes? Would it take a great deal of strength?'

'No, just as I said, a strong heart. Firmness of purpose, you say in English.'

Phryne got out her small mirror and examined the faint red fingermarks on her delicate skin, already fading. 'That's where the black bruises were. Exactly like that. She's dead, Lin, someone killed her, and then someone took the body. I don't understand. But I will. Now, there have been other developments, too. Someone came into my room while I was asleep – a man, that's all I can say.'

'There might be many reasons to come to your room, Silver Lady,' his voice was amused.

'Yes, and that's what my previous visitor Gerald had in mind, but the second one – I don't know, Lin, I didn't want him to find me. I can't explain, but I was sure I did not want to be discovered and that he did not intend amorous dalliance. This place is giving me the grues, as Dot would say.'

'I have also had an occurrence, Phryne,' said Lin Chung evenly. 'When my valet came to lay out my evening clothes, he found something on my dressing-table which had not been there when we went to lunch.'

'Oh? What?' Phryne declined to guess. In Cave House, it could be anything from a golden bee from the Empress Josephine's dress to a fresh plate of *soupe printanière* made with real springs.

'An urn,' said Lin Chung. 'I believe there are a lot of them in the house – you'd think the English would understand the Chinese better, we both have ancestor-worship – and some maid may have brought it there by mistake.'

'That sounds very unlikely. Where is it now?'

'Li Pen replaced it. It was a rather handsome one, marble with a gilded lid. It stood on a plinth in the hall, and now it is back there.'

'Did anyone see Li Pen replace it?'

'I doubt it. Li Pen has made something of a profession of not being noticed.'

'Don't let me go, and to Hell with my reputation, I'm cold,' said Phryne, snuggling closer. There was something infinitely reliable about Lin Chung, and moreover he was very warm. The heat of his skin was palpable.

'What do you make of the urn?' she asked.

'A joke, I fancy,' said Lin slowly, allowing one hand to cup Phryne's chilled face. 'Not a very funny one. Is there more?'

'Certainly,' she said, and told him all that she could recall about the assignation in the library, mentioning the presence of the poet and Miss Medenham. She added the whole tale of Tom Reynolds and Jack Lucas's father and the argument about the inheritance.

'Most interesting.'

'You're being inscrutable again,' accused Phryne.

'So solly, Missee,' he apologised and Phryne reached up to clip his ears. He caught her wrist and she twisted her hand free, not amused.

'Enough of the stage Chinaman. It disconcerts me, stop it. Now, what are we to do? Do we tell anyone?'

'How can we? I believe you, Silver Lady, but it is unlikely that anyone else will, because you are telling them something they do not want to hear.'

'True,' agreed Phryne. 'But I need to know what

happened. We have sufficient resources to solve the riddle between us, Lin dear. Let us consider. I saw the Doctor come out of that room just after lunch. He said that Lina would be awake at tea. That's now and we are missing it. Can you manage without tea?'

'I would walk many miles to sit under a tree with you, Silver Lady – and to miss English tea, which is not tea as I know it.'

'Good. I saw the Doctor about one-thirty. By three-thirty the girl is dead. And by three-forty, at the most, the body is gone and the room tidied.'

'Yes. The timing is rather strict. What is the next question?'

'Who wanted her dead? She seems to have been a harmless, if addled, girl.'

'Too many novels,' agreed Lin Chung. 'Li Pen tells me that in the kitchen they say that she was curious about everything, too fond of sweets, especially chocolate, and prone to spin fancies about the guests. Mrs Croft says that she doted on the poet, but I don't know how far the affair progressed, if there was one. There was only minor resentment about her being the housekeeper's niece, so she must have been an adroit girl.'

'And now she's dead,' said Phryne. She stared across the lawn at the grey, roiling river, and thought angrily of Lina who had eaten her last chocolate, ripped out of life by someone's strong hands around her throat. Had she woken and seen the face of her attacker, died hard and in terror, or slipped out of life without a sigh, unconscious in one minute and suffocated in five? Either way, it was intolerable.

'We must find out where everyone was between one-thirty and three-thirty. Where were you?'

'I concluded my game of tennis with Miss Fletcher at about two-fifteen and went to my room to change. Then I looked for you and could not find you, so I sat down in the small parlour to read *Bleak House*. I stayed there until you came in looking like a spirit.'

'Did anyone else pass through?'

'Yes, several people. Miss Mead was in the room for a while, just after I got there, talking to Mrs Fletcher about crochet. Mr Reynolds and the Major, I believe, went fishing. Mrs Reynolds was in the adjoining parlour talking to the cook about menus – I could hear her.'

'Yes, I saw her there. I didn't look into the little parlour, Lin. Is that where you were? I saw the poet and Miss Cynthia in the library – that place was designed for assignations. Ask Li Pen to find out about the menservants, and Dot can locate the ladies. I mean to see this solved, Lin.'

'Why?' he asked. It was not an idle question. Phryne thought about it.

'Because it is disgusting. I didn't take to poor Lina, but someone killed her and they are not getting away with it. Also, taking into account the man in my room and the shot in the mist, it might be us, next. This house feels dangerous. Will you help me?'

'Yes,' said Lin Chung. 'I'll help you.'

Phryne and Lin Chung came back into the house as afternoon tea was being cleared away. The company was all gathered in the parlour. Phryne retraced her steps to Lina's room, up the grand staircase and then the hidden one.

'Look,' she exclaimed. 'Can you see footprints?'

Lin Chung leaned down and outlined a muddy mark on the stair carpet. 'A boot – a man's boot,' he commented.

'Yes, and they go all the way to Lina's room, two tracks – coming and going.'

Lin walked down to the nearest guestroom, which happened to be Phryne's, and pressed a buzzer. When a panting maid appeared, he said, 'Send my manservant to me, please.'

'Wait,' Phryne interposed. 'You're the chambermaid, aren't you, responsible for the rooms?' The girl nodded. She was a solid young person with short blond hair and round blue eyes like a doll's. 'Did you change Lina's bed just now?'

'Why, yes, Miss. I was doing the rooms and saw that she wasn't there, so I made her bed and cleaned the room. Why, is anything wrong, Miss?'

'No, of course, what could be wrong?' replied Phryne. 'Was the window open?'

'No, Miss, I opened it. Let in some fresh air, like. Missus' orders.'

'Good. That's all,' said Phryne, and the girl sped down the back staircase for the kitchen, where presumably Li Pen was taking tea with the rest of the domestics.

'Why do we want Li Pen?'

'He can tell me about the footprints. Silver Lady, Li Pen is a great hunter. They call him "Tiger-slayer" in his village because he once followed and killed a man-eater. Hunters track things.'

Lin Chung removed himself punctiliously from Phryne's room and she leaned in the doorway.

'Confucian principles holding out?' she asked, sweetly.

'Just,' he admitted, taking in the invitation in her stance.

'Drat,' said Phryne, not noticeably annoyed.

Li Pen and Dot answered the summons. Lin spoke briefly in Cantonese to his valet, and Li Pen's smooth face seemed to sharpen, though his features remained unmoved. He dropped to the floor at the foot of the small staircase, his nose almost touching the carpet, then inched his way up.

'Break a snake's back to follow him,' said Dot. 'What's this all about, Miss?'

'I'll tell you later, Dot dear. Just now we've found some footprints. Who wears hobnailed boots?'

'Gardener and his boy, Miss, and that Mr Willis who used to be a jockey. The mechanic might, but in any case they wouldn't wear 'em in the house, Miss. Mrs Croft won't allow boots in her kitchen, they've all got slippers by the door.'

'Have they, indeed. Dot, you are invaluable.'

'Miss, you think something's happened to Lina, don't you?'

Phryne looked into Dot's worried eyes. 'Yes,

Dot, I do think that something happened to her. What's the consensus in the kitchen?'

'No one knows what to think, Miss. The Hinchcliffs haven't seen her since this morning. Mrs H thinks she might have wandered off, being troubled in her mind. Mr H isn't saying anything. They say Mr Reynolds is going to organise a search party for Lina but they're afraid that . . . with the river so high . . .'

'Yes.' They had followed Lin Chung's straight back and Li Pen's snaking feet up the stair. Now they stood outside Lina's door. Li Pen had his hand on his master's arm and was speaking vehemently in short hissing sentences.

'Li Pen says,' translated Lin, 'that the booted feet came up fast and unladen, and went down more slowly, carrying something heavy. He says that he can follow them down, too.'

'Then you do that while Dot and I examine this room. Now, Dot dear, I'm relying on you. The room's been cleaned, but there still might be some clues. Have a look around.'

'You think that she's dead, don't you, Miss Phryne?' she said quietly. Phryne nodded. Dot drew a deep breath. 'Well, Miss, the blanket's new, the bed's been made by an expert; probably Doreen, she's the chambermaid. Look, mitred corners.' Dot pulled the whole bedstead aside and poked at the corner of the rug. 'This is where she'd hide anything she had to keep secret, Miss. See, there's a tack missing out of the carpet. The corner comes up easily.' She lifted it and groped underneath. 'There, Miss.' She gave Phryne a small box which had once held Empire Toffee.

'Good, anything else?'

'Nothing in the wardrobe, Miss, just a heavy coat and the usual clothes. Nothing much in her box, either, except a towel that's marked "Cave House" and her washing things.'

Phryne sorted swiftly through a pile of paperback novels by the reading lamp. Sinister yellow faces leered from the cover of *Dope* and *Limehouse Nights*. Phryne took up each book by the spine and shook it, yielding a forest of chocolate wrappers (Lina favoured soft centres), scrap paper and bus tickets. Poor Lina, who had loved sweets and sensational literature. No wonder she had panicked when she saw Li Pen. Phryne gathered all the bookmarks. Dot held out her hands to receive the debris and forced it into her cardigan pocket.

'Come on, let's see how our sleuth-hound is doing,' Phryne said, and they left the small cold room, empty now of the merest signs of occupation.

They encountered Tom at the back door, watching Li Pen and his master walking in single file through a wilderness of cabbages.

'They say the girl was carried out of my house,' said Tom. 'Nonsense. I don't believe in all this Red Indian "white man speaks with forked tongue" gobbledy-gook.'

'I might point out, Tom dear, that the tracker is

actually Chinese and so far hasn't shown any signs of speaking pidgin English. Lina is gone, Tom. How do you explain that?'

'Girl's off her head. She's run away,' said Tom stoutly.

'Oh yes, in bare feet and nightdress? Excuse me, I'd better go and join Chief Lin and his Indian scout. Come on, Dot.'

'Miss ...' Dot whispered in Phryne's ear, 'I might be more use in the servants' hall.'

'So you might. Go and have a cuppa and a nice sit down, Dot,' said Phryne.

Leaving Tom on the threshold, a picture of landed gentry in exquisite discomfort, she followed the path through the kitchen garden and caught up with Lin and Li Pen as they traced the heavy nailed boots to the stables.

'Lost him,' said Lin, as Li Pen stared down at a flat expanse of mud, churned up by hoofs. 'We'll cast around the edge.'

'Go on,' said Phryne. 'I'll have a word with the stablemen.'

The stables were well built, well littered and sound. They smelt agreeably of horses, straw and leather-dressing with a faint whiff of Stockholm Tar, a compound of lard and black sulphur. Phryne patted Cuba's nose, noticing that his knees were bandaged with skill.

Mr Willis approached crab-wise and commented, "E's sparky, is Cuba. I reckon 'e'll be bonzer in a couple of weeks. What can I do for you, Miss?'

'Lina's missing,' said Phryne, looking straight at

the stableman even though both hands were occupied in gentling the noble head. 'Boot prints lead from the house to the stables. What do you know about it, eh?'

'Nothin' – I don't know nothin'.' He avoided her eyes. 'Missin', is she? Must'a gone off 'er nut.'

'Possibly. However just to be careful, you are going to search the stables and make sure that she didn't run away and hide here. It's cold and she only has a nightgown on.'

'Boss know you're 'ere?' he asked suspiciously.

'Boss knows,' said Tom Reynolds heavily, appearing behind her. 'Get on with it, Terry.'

Phryne and Tom followed as the jockey began at one corner of the building and, pitchfork in hand, probed every wisp of straw in the place. His attendant boy moved the horses from their stalls and held them in the cold corridor as Phryne watched the fork stab down, hitting asphalt with a grating screech each time. It was a trying noise and by the time the stable, the stableman's quarters and the baled hay had been searched, she had an ache in her jaw from gritting her teeth and stable dust liberally coating her person.

'Right, Terry, thanks. We've got to cover everywhere. If you see the poor wench, hang on to her and call the house right away,' said Tom.

They left the stable. Lin Chung was out of sight, down the bank towards the river. Phryne heard him yell, 'This way!' and Tom Reynolds groaned, 'Oh, no, not the river . . .'

They mounted the bank and went down to

where the two Chinese stood on the brink of a grey torrent. There was no sign of the bundle of nightdress which Phryne had feared to see.

'The tracks give out here,' said Lin Chung. 'Li Pen says that either the booted man walked into the river or he doubled back. The grass is green and springy, very hard to read.'

'He can't have walked into that,' said Phryne, watching as a packing case whisked past at a good twenty knots and vanished around the bend. 'No one could swim in that water.'

'No. But a body, thrown in at this point, would not beach until it reached the main river – perhaps not even then,' said Lin.

Tom Reynolds, who had been enpurpling for some minutes, exploded.

'Ridiculous! The girl isn't dead! She's gone off her head and run away. I'm organising a search party; we'll comb the grounds. We'll find her. Now I've got to go and muster the men.'

He stomped off. Li Pen looked at Lin Chung and said something which caused Lin to laugh shortly.

'He says that only the guilty are so angry.'

'Not necessarily. Tom thought you'd found her and was so relieved that you hadn't that he lost his temper,' commented Phryne. 'Could you thank Li Pen properly for me? He must have been a great hunter.'

To her surprise, Li bowed and said in his hesitant English, 'It is my pleasure to serve you, Lady.'

Phryne smiled. Lin Chung took her hand.

'Li, go back to the house and watch and listen,' he ordered. 'Phryne, will you walk with me?' Li Pen bowed and departed.

'Aren't you joining Tom's search party?' asked Phryne, conscious of the warm hand enclosing her own.

'Yes, but they must come this way. And we know that they are not going to find anything.' He drew her away from the swollen river and along the bank which hid it from the house.

'We have searched Lina's room,' said Phryne. 'She took no clothes and all her shoes are there. And I know she is dead.'

'Could you have been mistaken? Did you touch her? Was she cold?'

'No, I didn't go into the room. But she was blue, Lin – swollen and blue. No living creature looks like that.'

'Hmm.' He thought about it.

'We have no more facts to exchange,' she said. 'I'm cold. Let's go back to the house.'

'In a moment, Silver Lady.' He stopped and turned to her. 'In the presence of death we cling closer to life, to the flesh and the spirit, fearing dissolution.'

'True,' she agreed, leaning into his warmth as a skilled hand slid down to caress her breast, sensitive to touch even through her parrot-patterned jumper.

'I have said that I will not lie with you under our host's roof.' His mouth was almost touching her ear, his breath warm on her neck.

'Yes, I heard you,' Phryne noticed that her voice was quavering and dragged herself under control. Almost without volition, her hands slipped under the silk shirt and caressed a back as smooth as sun-warmed marble.

'But there are other places,' he said, almost inaudibly, and Phryne felt a jolt shoot through her spine.

'So there are,' she said, forcing her voice to become light. 'We shall reconnoitre. Too late for tonight, Lin dear. It's already getting dark. I think it's going to storm again.'

She was only taken marginally by surprise when he bent his head and kissed her passionately, soft mouth and silken lips, and the back muscles trembled reflexively under her fingers.

He drew away from her only as they heard the trampling feet of the search party approaching.

She had a lot to think about as she went back to the house. As she entered under the stone portal, it began to rain.

CHAPTER SEVEN

Oblivion is not to be hired.

Urn Burial, Sir Thomas Browne, Chapter V.

PHRYNE WAS dressing for dinner. The search party, defeated by the weather and the approach of night, had returned wet and grumbling. They had found no trace of Lina. It was pouring outside the bow windows, a steady drumming against the glass. Phryne yawned. Rain made her sleepy. She had bathed and was wearing her padded silk robe, a present from Lin Chung. Splashes of bright gold chrysanthemums across a background of dark-green leaves cheered her, and the silk wadding was as warm as fur. The smooth fabric caressed her skin like a hand.

She was sitting in her Sheridan chair, feet towards the fire, staring at the vague oil painting which had been in Dot's room. It was an improvement on *Hope*. Ladies with parasols were walking down a flower-strewn slope towards the artist.

There was a breeze; their hair was blown back and one parasol had turned inside out. Although filthy from long exposure to soot – it must have hung over a mantelpiece – it had a certain internal light which Phryne felt she had seen before, somewhere. She idled with the idea but could not pin it down. Europe, somewhere. A French voice came back to her, talking about clarity.

Dot came in briskly, turned on the light, and the impression vanished.

'Dinner, Miss,' she said. 'What would you like to wear?'

'The jade dress, I think. It's cold.' Phryne dismissed her train of thought and watched as Dot laid out the gown of the season.

Being a dinner dress, it was only ankle length. The fishtail train on Phryne's ball dress, which seemed, sadly, to be unlikely to see society, at least at this party – was designed for dancing and to overawe the servants. It also provided a convenient test for a clumsy young man to demonstrate just how awkward he was, thus saving Phryne's feet from many a trampling. If he stood on the train she didn't dance with him. Dot smoothed the velvet and fluffed up the squirrel-fur collar and cuffs, then found gunmetal-coloured stockings and the silver shoes.

Phryne donned black silk underwear and allowed Dot to drop the dress over her head. She made up her face with a few precise licks of a powder compact, sketched in her eyebrows, painted her mouth, shook her fluid hair into place and surveyed herself narrowly in the wardrobe mirror.

The jade-green velvet, cut by a master, flowed from the furry collar down to her neat ankles and well-shod feet. Phryne turned and walked, watching the movement of the fabric. Beautiful. The dress depended from her shapely shoulders. It was decorously cut, more from considerations of pneumonia than morality, with a high neck and no unseemly display of vertebrae. Poitou had sent it from Paris with his personal compliments to *la belle Anglaise*, and Phryne thought that he would have been pleased with it. The gown draped over her body, emphasising just what she wanted emphasised, and was remarkably decent while having a wholly indecent effect.

Dot set a fillet onto the black hair. It had a small panache of seagull's feathers caught in an ornate silver clip. Phryne slid onto her left middle finger the big silver ring she had bought in Shanghai, the dragon and the phoenix, symbolising the mating of yin and yang, male and female, sun and moon, darkness and light.

'Perfect,' she said, and smiled at her reflection. It smiled back. 'What's the news from the kitchen, Dot?'

'Mrs Croft thinks Lina's run away and so do most of the others. Mr Hinchcliff is worried, though – so's his wife. We only see them at dinner, Miss. Mr Reynolds ordered that all the outside staff have dinner at six. He says they work hard and need their food. We'll eat after you do, Miss.

Looks like a good dinner, too. Mr H hardly ate anything and Mrs H has been crying. Doreen says there was nothing strange about the room, except that the bottom sheet and the blanket were missing, so she put new ones on the bed. She's upset because she reckons she must have missed Lina by a minute and might have been able to help her.'

'She couldn't have helped her, Dot,' said Phryne soberly.

'You think she's dead, Miss. Why?'

'I saw her dead. All Doreen has done is spare herself a dreadful sight.'

Dot was silent. 'I don't s'pose we can just go away, Miss?' she asked hopefully.

'Not a chance,' said Phryne. The reflection's red mouth hardened into a straight line and the green eyes narrowed. Dot sighed.

'I was afraid you were going to say that, Miss Phryne.'

'I don't think we're in too much danger, Dot, but after you come back from dinner, shove a chair-back under the doorknob. I'll knock when I come. Just in case, Dot dear,' she said hastily. 'The door doesn't seem to have a key.'

'Not only that, Miss, it hasn't even got a latch. I had a look at it earlier. The lock's not working.'

'How singular,' Phryne observed. 'The good old chair it is then. Now don't worry, Dot. I'd better go down. Enjoy your dinner and keep an ear out for gossip. Find out what everyone was doing before they came here, if you can. I'm especially curious about that remarkable couple, the Hinch-cliffs. They're not the sort of people I would expect to find in the backblocks. Be good.' Phryne kissed Dot. 'I'm relying on you.'

Dot said, 'Yes, Miss,' and waited until Phryne had gone in a waft of Jicky before wiping the lipstick mark off her cheek.

'You're enough to drive me mental,' said Dot to the closed door. 'But you smell so nice.'

Dinner, it appeared, was going to be testing. The gathering in the drawing room was nervous: Miss Cray was muttering prayers in an annoying undertone, Miss Mead was looking like someone who had just discovered the Mother's Club rehearsing the Black Mass instead of the Wednesday Play, Tom Reynolds had taken more brandy than was good for him and the poet had not only matched but exceeded his consumption. Mrs Reynolds' brow was furrowed, Lin Chung looked absolutely expressionless, Miss Fletcher was talking too loudly about the leg-before-wicket rule, Gerald looked crumpled and Jack Lucas short-tempered. The Major's shirt front was ballooning out as he declaimed that all women were pests and a curse and no time need be wasted on such a light-headed, irresponsible, fundamentally wicked sex.

'It's not money that's the root of all evil, but women,' he declared. His wife, wispy in pale-blue, cowered away from him and Doctor Franklin, who was the main recipient of the Major's discourse, looked harried. Only Mrs Fletcher looked pleased, and that might have been because Judith was leaning ostentatiously on Gerald's arm. Miss Medenham was remarkable in cyclamen chiffon and amethysts. The poet was offering her a cocktail and drinking her in with what looked like serious, if alcoholically inspired, concentration.

The gentlemen were dressed in the usual panoply; the ladies ranged from Joan Fletcher's 'suitable' grey velvet to Miss Cray's habitual mourning weeds, dressed up with a multitude of jet brooches with hair in them.

Phryne swept in and Lin Chung detached himself from the gathering with deceptive ease and offered her his arm.

'You look absolutely beautiful,' he said softly. Phryne surveyed him. His clothes, she thought, were made to measure in Savile Row, or perhaps in Oxford. They fitted him like a glove. The linen irreproachable; the links and studs of round undecorated gold in very good taste. His hair was as shiny as patent leather and he was as sleek and self-satisfied as a black cat.

'So do you,' she told him with perfect truth.

'Shall we go in?' asked the hostess. Phryne accepted Tom Reynolds' arm. As the highest-ranking lady, it was her place to go first and be seated first.

Tom was more than a trifle unsteady as the great doors opened into a dining room shining with glass and lit by three chandeliers. The tables were laid with damask as white as snow, on which were displayed glasses in the highest state of gleam; silver polished to extinction, several epergnes full of ferns and a real Sevres dinner service – Peninsular War vintage. Unless it came with the house, it must have cost Tom several fortunes. Phryne hoped that the domestics knew that the penalty for dropping a plate was a shooting at dawn.

She paraded down the length of the room. The decor was, as usual, mixed. Linen-fold panelling lined the walls, but the ceiling was decorated with a frieze of dancing Greek maidens and plaster mouldings in the shape of trailing bunches of ivy and grapes. A Dionysiad, therefore; but a very polite one. No nymph could get into too much trouble when she had such a very tight corset on under her tunic. The floor was parquet and slightly springy, and the windows were draped with full High Victorian curtains, endless falls of heavy velvet and piles of priceless lace heaped carelessly to the floor.

'Lord, Tom, what a room,' she murmured, holding her host up with a hand under his elbow.

'Magnificent, ain't it?' he blurred.

'I've never seen anything like it. Come along, old thing, you're meant to sit here, the head of the table, and I sit here on your left. Downsy-daisy,' said Phryne, pushing slightly as the butler shoved the chair forward. Hinchcliff flourished his master's napkin and spread it on his lap. Phryne exchanged a rueful glance with him. How had

Tom got so polluted in such a short time? Although the large man's face remained perfectly butlerine, she caught a flicker of a wink and a small, very fleeting, smile.

'That's the way,' she encouraged. 'You have to have something to eat, Tom dear. You shouldn't drink on an empty stomach.'

''M not drunk,' protested Tom.

'No, of course not, my dear,' said Phryne, very pleased that Lin Chung was sitting beside her with Miss Medenham and Jack Lucas opposite. At least she would have someone to talk to.

The rest of the company had entered, each gentleman escorting a lady, and Phryne looked down the board. She could not see far, because of a bank of ferns of Amazonian luxuriance. The Major had been separated from his wife, who was sitting next to Tadeusz. Luttrell was inflicting his opinions on Joan Fletcher who, by the look of her, was about to deliver a mustard-plaster snub. Phryne hoped that she would be able to hear it. Miss Cray and Miss Mead flanked the Doctor, and Gerald Randall had accompanied Judith Fletcher and was even listening to what she was saying, or appearing to. Perhaps, Phryne thought, he really was interested in cricket.

'Hock, Madam?' asked Mr Hinchcliff, and Phryne nodded. Perhaps Tom Reynolds was wise. This assortment of people might look much better through the pink spectacles of the slightly shickered. She examined the menu card, written in waiter's French.

Pure Mrs Beeton. No one would serve a meal of such richness and variety in the city now, except possibly the Lord Mayor. Phryne sipped the hock, hoped that she was hungry, and joined in politely to Lin Chung's conversation about Oxford.

The delights of that city lasted through the *consommé de gibier*, game soup composed mostly of local rabbit and possibly pigeon.

'I suppose that it is difficult to make game soup in Australia,' she commented, 'though this is excellent. No partridges or quail, no wild birds.'

'There's a recipe for parrot soup,' Tom Reynolds came awake. 'You take an old boot and a couple of parrots. You put them in a pot and stew them until the old boot is soft. Then you throw the parrots away and eat the old boot.'

Having delivered himself of this culinary gem, Tom lapsed into his reverie again.

'Well, they are so decorative that I wouldn't want to eat them anyway,' said Miss Medenham with aplomb. 'Don't you agree, Miss Fisher? I saw a flight of galahs from my window this afternoon, like a grey cloud. Then they turned, and the cloud was pink.'

'They are beautiful,' agreed Phryne. 'And as you say, very *Art décoratif*. Those bold colours – black and crimson, or the red, blue and gold of rosellas.'

'Greenfinches would make a lovely frieze around a room,' said Jack Lucas. 'Flights and flights of green birds, or silver-eyes, perhaps, in that strange grey-green like gumleaves.'

'Or that chalk-blue of budgies, though perhaps

not a frieze,' commented Lin Chung. 'The feathers are very fine. Promise me, Phryne, you will not start a fashion? If you wear the bright plumage, all the ladies will emulate you and there will not be a parrot left in Australia, which would be a pity.'

'I promise,' Phryne smiled. 'The feathers I'm wearing are from a seagull, and I picked them up myself on Elwood beach after he had preened them away. Dot put them together – she is a famous needlewoman.'

'They are quite perfect,' said Jack Lucas. 'They seem to set off your silky black hair just as Miss Medenham's amethysts set off her golden locks.'

'Do you admire my golden locks, Jack?' asked Miss Medenham, shaking her head so that all of her purple stones flashed in the chandelier's bright light.

'You know I do,' he said.

There was a pause. The housemaid, moving with extreme care, offered fillets of trout cooked with almonds. The gentlemen had obviously caught some fish.

'Tom, dear, would you like some *truite almandine*?' asked Phryne as he stared blankly at the embarrassed maid. 'You caught them, you know.'

'Me? No. I never caught nothing. Fish, eh? No. Don't want no fish.'

Phryne waved a hand at the butler, who came instantly and leaned down so that she could whisper. He smelt of starch and eau-de-cologne.

'I think your master might improve with some

coffee. Strong, you know, and black. Can you sort of sneak it in so the others don't notice?' He nodded, gave her an approving look which left Phryne feeling a little overwhelmed, and went away.

The trout was delicious, though Phryne heard Miss Cray complaining that hers had not been cooked properly. Miss Mead, a sensible woman, explained the concept of *bleu* in an undertone, which did not stop Miss Cray from observing, 'How revolting!' at the top of her not inconsiderable voice.

Phryne let her hand slip under the table to meet Lin Chung's where it rested on his thigh. It was going to be a long night and according to the menu there were three courses yet to get through. He patted her hand consolingly.

'Tell me, Miss Fisher, how have the cases been going? Miss Fisher's a famous detective,' added Miss Medenham in explanation. Phryne began to tell the story of the cast of *Ruddigore* and the ghost. It was a good story and she told it with appropriate verve, so that Jack Lucas was fascinated and even Tom was listening.

'She's a clever girl, this one,' he said thickly, as she reached the end. 'Clever girl. Even though she brought a Chinese lover. I don't mind that, why should I? I knew a Chinese girl once. Her name was Soong – Song, that was it, she was a song. That was in Hong Kong, before the war. Pretty little thing. What's this, Hinchcliff? I didn't ask for this.' The butler was offering him a breakfast cup such as is used for soup. The butler did not reply but stood fixed and immovable, looking permanent. Hinchcliff, Phryne felt, would stand there with that cup until Tom drank it or the heavens fell, whichever came first.

'You just drink it and don't argue,' said Cynthia Medenham, unexpectedly firm. Tom gazed fuzzily in her direction and observed, 'Blondes. Blondes are strong-minded women.'

'Quite right, my dear. I am strong-minded, so drink up. You should know better than to argue with a blonde, an old newspaperman like you,' she said, and Tom reached over, tried to pinch her cheek, missed, and swallowed the coffee in one complicated movement. His eyes, for a moment, opened wide. Phryne reflected that it must have been concentrated caffeine.

The saddle of mutton was brought in with some ceremony. There were boiled potatoes and cabbage in butter to accompany this. Phryne was wondering what on earth to do. The host was supposed to carve and she would not have liked to be within knife's reach of a drunken Tom Reynolds, who was given to wide, all-encompassing gestures. He might not mean to slash pieces off his guests, but he might do it nonetheless. She resolved to dive under the table at the first sign of mayhem.

But Mr Hinchcliff knew his duty. The mutton had been meticulously sliced in the kitchen, and the housemaid was carrying the platter in triumph along the table before the master noticed that he had been supplanted.

From the end of the table where convention had

trapped her, too far away for effective action, Evelyn Reynolds stared at Phryne with desperate eyes, begging her to do something.

Phryne let go of Lin Chung's hand and said to Tom, 'These are excellent potatoes. Do you grow them?'

'Yes,' said Tom, blinking. 'The soil's perfect for potatoes, we got three truckloads out of the north field last year. Lucky, too. You can live on potatoes. Look at all those Irishmen. We might have to, if the river rises any higher.'

'I'm sure that your wife has the catering well in hand, Tom,' soothed Phryne.

'Yes, m'wife is a capable woman, capable. Pity about the boy. She'd have been different if the boy had turned out well. But he went to the bad. Lots of boys do, you know. I went to the bad myself.'

'Tom, do shut up,' said Phryne.

'Ah, Jack.' He noticed Jack Lucas for the first time. 'Nice boy, Jack. So was his father. His father was a nice boy. Man.'

'Have some cabbage,' urged Miss Medenham nervously. 'Do you grow the cabbages, too?'

'Cabbages,' said Tom owlishly. 'Babies grow under cabbages, eh, don't they? Eh, Annie? Did you find them under a cabbage?'

This pronouncement caused the housemaid to drop the dish, clap both hands to her face, and run blindly out of the room. Tom Reynolds gaped after her.

While there was a certain fascination in anticipating what he might say next, Phryne drew the line at cruelty. 'Tom, you must pull yourself together,' she said in a fierce undertone. 'You're drunk and you're babbling. Stop it at once. I'm ashamed of you.'

'I'm ashamed of me, too,' his face fell and he looked like he was going to cry. Phryne looked around for help. Hinchcliff materialised at her side.

'I'm afraid that Mr Reynolds is ill,' she said flatly. 'He has caught a chill. Lin darling – would you mind?'

Tom was minded to protest, but Lin caught him in an unbreakable hold and he and the butler escorted him firmly out of the dining room.

'How did old Tom get that drunk that fast?' asked Cynthia. 'I've never seen him so plastered.'

'I expect he's worried about Lina. What do you think happened to her?'

'My dear,' Miss Medenham leaned forward conspiratorially, 'they haven't found a trace of her, except for that trail of boots that your Mr Lin's man followed. He sounds exciting. Is he really a hunter?'

'Yes, he's called "tiger-slayer" and he can track like a hound.' Phryne also leaned closer.

'I'd love a tiger skin. To lie on, you know.' Miss Medenham had obviously been reading Elinor Glyn and her own fiction. 'But about the maid, it's too spooky. I'm locking my door tonight, I can tell you. It might be that old tramp, that Dingo Harry. But what does he want with her? It's too deliciously exciting.'

A vision of the girl's dead face rose before Phryne's eyes and she gulped the remains of her hock. Jack Lucas said, 'You think something awful happened to Lina, don't you? Well, it won't be old Dingo Harry. He's a red-ragger. If he was breaking into houses and stealing girls, it would be one of the ladies, not an oppressed daughter of the labouring classes.'

Miss Medenham suppressed a shriek and Phryne said, 'That sounds familiar,' as the returning Mr Hinchcliff filled a glass with claret and set it before her. Lin Chung sat down again and nodded at Phryne's inquiring glance. 'I know a couple of wharfies who think like that.' She suddenly missed Bert and Cec and wished that she had them here. They were infinitely reliable. What they would have made of Cave House would have been worth hearing, also. She imagined the stocky Bert taking off his hat and saying, 'Strewth!' and Cec behind him echoing, 'Too right', and felt immediately better.

'You know this Dingo Harry then?' breathed Miss Medenham, hoping not to be disappointed of her monster.

'He's all for the working man,' said Jack. 'Gerry and I used to meet him quite often at the caves. He knows all about them. He used to be a geologist, then the grog got him and he came out here, prospecting. That fell through and he makes a living out of dingo trapping. He likes caves. He says there's miles of them, all through the hills, and tunnels and seams of metals and maybe even ores. Best-educated swaggie I ever met. He looks a bit wild and woolly but he's all right. I can't imagine him hurting anyone.'

'Then who was it?' Cynthia accepted a piece of lemon tart and poured cream onto it with a distracted hand.

'Don't know,' said Jack Lucas shortly.

'Tell me what you think of the decor,' said Phryne, searching for another topic. The young man smiled and his blue eyes lit with mirth.

'It's amazing, isn't it? It can't really date, because it's such a mixture. I mean, the medieval panelling and the marble fireplaces and those magnificent Morris windows.'

'Are any of the antiques really antique?'

'Oh, yes. The original owner bought up big at the Paris Exhibition. The settle in the hall is fifteenth-century. The big chippendale table in the parlour is genuine, as is the Sheridan love-seat in gold-coloured satin in the little parlour. These are real Sevres plates, ghastly as they are, the whole set from soup to dessert. Have you got a battle on yours?'

Phryne scraped away the *gelée au citron* to ascertain. 'Yes, Salamanca.'

'I've got Albuera,' said Miss Medenham.

'You're lucky – I've got a portrait of Blücher, enough to sour cream.' Jack poured some over his *charlotte russe* in a spirit of scientific enquiry.

'So this would be your profession, would it?' asked Phryne. 'Antiques?'

'I never thought of it, actually,' he said, holding

a spoonful suspended in the air. 'I suppose it could be.'

'Think about it,' said Phryne, suddenly remembering a French voice talking about plain air. 'I think I can see a way out of your little difficulty, Mr Lucas.'

'You can?'

'I think so, but perhaps we can talk about it another day. There is no hurry. What about you, Miss Medenham? Are you interested in antiques?'

'My dear, I just had my flat entirely renovated and threw all of the old things away. I want something madly *moderne*, frightfully gay. It's all colours, all angles, even the chairs are cubes.'

'What did you do with your old furniture?' asked Jack.

'I sold it to a rag-and-bone man, my dear. I just wanted the space. Now I've got oodles of light and air, free of all that heavy brass and cedar and mahogany.'

'I see,' said Jack Lucas.

Mrs Reynolds cast her glance around the table and rose.

'Lord, I forgot about leaving the gentlemen to their port,' exclaimed Phryne. 'Come on, Miss Medenham. You can tell me all about your new flat.'

'I've got red walls in the parlour,' said Miss Medenham as the gentlemen rose with a scraping of chairs. The ladies filed out, and Mr Hinchcliff put two crystal decanters on the table.

The drawing room contained the apparatus for

coffee and tea and small plates of nuts and biscuits. Phryne listened with half an ear to Cynthia's extremely detailed description of her new furniture and eavesdropped shamelessly on the other conversations.

Judith was sulkily drinking coffee and trying not to hear her mother's lecture on proper behaviour. Phryne heard, 'You'll never catch a young man if you continue to beat them at tennis,' before deciding that she could guess the rest and passed on. Miss Cray had sought her virtuous couch early and Miss Mead was sitting next to Letty Luttrell, discussing – of all things – adulterous love. Phryne edged her chair closer.

'But it was a very sad book,' Letty was saying. 'She had to go back to her husband and he had to go back to his wife.'

'They had obligations and had taken vows,' said Miss Mead gently.

'But do vows have to bind forever?' asked Letty. 'What if one finds that one has made a mistake, a dreadful mistake?'

'The Church says one has to stay. Even the most brutal husband must be obeyed, they say.'

Miss Mead turned a heel on the small fluffy bootee she was knitting and Letty said in a fierce whisper, 'I know what the Church says. What do you say?'

'I say, leave him if you can, my dear,' said Miss Mead unexpectedly.

This caught Miss Medenham's attention also. She broke off her enumeration of her new cubist cutlery and said incredulously, '*What* did you say, Miss Mead?'

'I said that a brutal husband need not be endured.' The skilled hands continued to knit, the thread looping exactly over the centre of the crossed needles. 'Why, what is your opinion, Miss Medenham?'

'I think the same. Can you leave him, Letty?'

'I . . . don't know.' Mrs Luttrell was taken aback by being the centre of all this conversation. Even Joan Fletcher had ceased berating her daughter to listen. 'I think he'd kill me if I tried.'

'Oh, come now, Letty, you're exaggerating,' scoffed Cynthia. Letty, for answer, pulled back the loose sleeves of her pale-blue woollen gown. The delicate wrists and thin forearms were marked across with black bruises. Phryne felt ill.

'God, Letty, how long has he been doing that?'

'He was kind when he wanted me to marry him,' said Letty quietly. 'He bought me violets, I remember. I've never been able to bear the scent of violets since. My boy was killed, you see, and I had nothing to live for and my mother has three daughters and he has a lot of money. Once we were married he changed. He's jealous. If I talk to a man, he questions me for hours, accuses me of all sorts of things.'

'And he beats you,' said Mrs Reynolds.

'Yes,' said Letty dismissively.

'But now there's another man,' said Judith excitedly.

Mrs Luttrell shrank, blushing bright-red. Phryne

restrained an urge to kick Miss Fletcher and said, 'We didn't mean to pry, Mrs Luttrell. Why don't you and Miss Mead go over to the piano to continue your discussion and we'll stay here. Would anyone like some more coffee?' Letty caught at her arm.

'No, no, it's all right,' she protested. 'You see, I've got no one to talk to. He doesn't like me to have friends. This is my only chance to talk. What should I do?'

'Have you got any money of your own?' asked Phryne. Letty shook her head. 'What about your lover?'

Letty looked doubtful. 'I don't think there's any money.'

'It might be an idea to find out, if you are serious,' said Miss Mead. 'You haven't any children, my dear – children make it difficult. But no one should stay and be tortured – the laws allow you to leave.'

Phryne knew that the laws might allow Mrs Luttrell to leave, but unless she intended passing the time between her departure and the decree absolute under medical supervision in a convent, the Major would declare to the Court that she was a loose woman and had deserted him without cause. Letty would find herself disgraced and out on the street without a sou or a sequin. However, even that might be better than being beaten and continually denigrated. Phryne was surprised to find that the browbeaten Mrs Luttrell had any spirit left at all.

'I want to run away,' said Letty plaintively. 'Miss Fletcher is right, there is someone. It's funny, really.' Her lips curved in a smile so sad that Phryne had to take a sip of Cointreau to still the pang. 'Will would never have brought me here if he had known.'

'Known what?' asked Miss Fletcher. Phryne moved into easy kicking distance of the young woman and resolved to apply her silver shoe without fear or favour at the very hint of another faux pas.

'Why, that my own darling is here,' said Mrs Luttrell. 'The one I love is here, in this house.'

CHAPTER EIGHT

Without confused burnings they affectionately
compounded their bones; passionately endeavouring
to continue their living unions.

Urn Burial, Sir Thomas Browne, Chapter III.

As it was clearly impossible to ask Mrs Luttrell
who her lover was – and Phryne caught Miss
Fletcher a shrewd blow on her shin when the question was hovering on her lips – there was not much
more to be said. The ladies drank their beverages,
Miss Fisher confining herself to Cointreau, and
they went in a body to the large parlour where a
gramophone was playing and the gentlemen
awaited them. They evidently had not lingered
over their port.

There were several distractions to while away
the long evening. The room was just big enough
to dance in, provided the dancers did not attempt
anything too athletic; Phryne remembered her
dancing-master telling her that one needed six

square yards in which to polka. There were the usual photograph albums, a scatter of the fashionable journals, and a very beautiful chess set, made of carved bone. The poet challenged the Doctor to a game. Miss Medenham walked boldly up to the Major and demanded a dance. Phryne wondered what on earth the combustible novelist thought she was doing, vamping a man who beat his wife. Then Lin Chung crossed her field of vision.

'This is a foxtrot,' he said. 'May I have this dance?' and Phryne floated into his embrace.

'How is Tom?' she asked.

'Drunk but affable. He was spouting family secrets like a geyser, wasn't he? Does he do this often?'

'No, I've never seen him like that before. You dance very well.'

'So do you.' Phryne saw Miss Mead seated by Mrs Fletcher. They looked amiably on. Even Mrs Fletcher seemed to have forgiven Lin Chung for being Chinese and charming, as her daughter Judith danced past with Gerry Randall. Jack Lucas had persuaded Mrs Reynolds to dance with him. They matched steps very well.

'You heard what he said,' Phryne reminded Lin. 'Tom said he had no objection to a love affair between you and me going on under his roof.'

'Even so,' said the smooth voice. 'He was not himself. There are other distractions, Silver Lady. Gerald is evidently overcome by your charms.'

'He's very pretty,' said Phryne consideringly. 'I'll think about it.'

'Not too much, I beg.' He broke step and then regained his rhythm.

'Oh? And are you intending to seduce the bouncing Miss Fletcher?' Lin laughed, unabashed. 'She said to me . . . she thinks . . .'

'Tell me.'

'She is under the impression that all Chinese men lust after white women. I had to find a way to disabuse her of this idea, while not telling her that to a Chinese she has hair like straw, round eyes like a demon, such eyes moreover the colour of a blind person or a devil, and lumps in all the wrong places.'

'Poor girl.'

'No, no, I was very polite.' He brought Phryne neatly round a corner. 'But you, Phryne, you are altogether different. If I had to explain your appeal I would have to say . . . I don't know what I would say. That you have the carriage of a Manchu Princess, the black hair and the neat head, the red mouth of a courtesan of the first rank, yet you have eyes like precious jade. Such eyes were never seen in China. That is what they would call you, the poets who came to make songs of your beauty. Green Jade, the Silver Lady. You are wearing your Shanghai ring.'

'The dragon and the phoenix, yes.'

'In Western philosophy they call it the alchemical marriage. The White Queen and the Red King. Their mating engenders the philosopher's stone.'

'The Major's wife wants to leave him,' said Phryne, changing the subject. If Lin Chung was to be coaxed out of his chastity, it would not be done by allowing him to enthuse endlessly about her beauty.

'Indeed? I can understand that.'

'She has a lover. Someone in this house. Can you hazard a guess?'

Lin considered the Doctor, the poet, Tom Reynolds, Gerald Randall and Jack Lucas, and shrugged fluidly.

'No, I cannot guess. Do you know?'

'No. Do any other groupings suggest themselves? Perhaps we can cancel them out like an equation.'

'What an immoral conversation,' observed Lin, amused. 'Let's see, Miss Medenham and the poet, I think. They were in the library together, you said. I think they'd be a match. Tom Reynolds and his wife seem devoted. The Major . . . no. I don't think any woman would find his bluster and bullying attractive.'

'Miss Medenham seems to,' said Phryne as the pair danced past, close together and talking.

'True. An eccentric woman – I believe that novelists often are,' said Lin. 'Well, perhaps Miss Fletcher and Gerald. And maybe I am wrong about Miss Medenham – I think she fancies Jack Lucas.'

'The woman fancies everyone. As you say, novelists. And Lucas is certainly good-looking. But very young.'

'You prefer experience, perhaps?' asked Lin, sliding a hand down the back of the velvet dress.

'Infinitely,' agreed Phryne, clasping his waist.

The gramophone whirled to a halt.

'Check and mate,' said the poet into the silence. 'You are off your game, Doctor.'

'Yes, Tadeusz, I don't feel well. I think I'll just sit here and play the gramophone.' The spare figure reached out a long hand and picked up the next record. 'Here's a Charleston.' He wound the machine up and placed the needle on the spinning wax platter.

'There is something macabre about the gramophone,' observed the poet. 'It preserves the voices of the dead, as cherries are preserved in confiture.'

'And are thus exalted,' commented Phryne. 'Jam is the highest state to which cherries can aspire. Good cherries become jam, and bad cherries become compost.'

The poet laughed.

'Down on your heels, up on your toes, stay after school, learn how it goes, that's the way to do the Varsity rag,' sang the gramophone.

The Charleston was not a complicated dance. It merely required strong ankles and good balance. Phryne could dance the Charleston all night.

She found herself next to Gerald. Two steps forward, two steps back. He was singing along with the next record.

'In olden days a glimpse of stocking was looked on as something shocking, now heaven knows, anything goes.'

'The world's mad today and good's bad today and black's white today and wrong's right today and most guys today that women prize today are just silly gigolos,' sang Phryne.

'Although I'm not a great romancer I know that you're bound to answer when I propose,' sang Gerald, staring into Phryne's eyes.

'Anything goes,' she replied. He really was a very pretty boy.

The Doctor, perhaps influenced by Mrs Reynolds' silent disapproval of modern dancing, put on a waltz. Gerald bowed and said, 'May I have this dance?' and Phryne smiled.

'Shouldn't you be dancing with Miss Fletcher?' she asked, moving closer to him. He was slim and smelt of port and the hand taking hers was smooth and strong.

'She doesn't waltz. In any case, I don't belong to her,' he said, his arm encircling Phryne's waist. 'I would much rather belong to you.'

To the sugary strains of 'The Blue Danube', Phryne waltzed with Gerald. Lin Chung was dancing with Mrs Reynolds. Jack Lucas had left the room. Letty Luttrell had presumably gone to bed. Judith was sitting next to the Doctor and leafing through the records. The poet had abandoned his surrealist principles and had led out Mrs Fletcher, and Miss Medenham was hanging on to the Major with grim determination.

'What does Miss Medenham see in the Major?' she asked idly, noticing that Gerald Randall was a very good dancer.

'God knows. Though I believe that she used to know him in Melbourne. She's rather marvellous, isn't she – so vivid.'

'Yes. You dance very well.'

'Only with you. You're as light as the feathers in your hair.'

Phryne smiled and noticed that her partner, who was leading, was moving them unobtrusively towards the door into the little parlour. As they passed under the carved Gothic lintel, the record wound to a close, but Gerald did not release his hold.

'Beautiful Phryne,' said the young man very softly. 'Most beautiful lady.'

'Exceptionally decorative Gerald,' she replied.

'Let me come to your room tonight,' he whispered. 'Last time, we were interrupted.'

'So we were,' she agreed. 'I'll think about it,' she temporised. 'This is a strange gathering and I'm worried about what happened to Lina. I don't know if I'm really in the mood, Gerald.'

'I can change your mood,' he said confidently.

'Can you, indeed? Perhaps,' she said. The music started again, a slow foxtrot, and Gerald gathered her close. There was little light in the small parlour, just a shaded pink lamp on one Victorian table. The bodies moved together, clung and slid, jade velvet against sable broadcloth.

Then they were no longer alone. Cynthia had manoeuvred the Major into the half-dark, her bright blond head leaning on his massive shoulder, and Gerald and Phryne slipped away, back into the general dance.

Before they parted, Phryne put her mouth to the young man's ear and breathed, 'Yes.'

Phryne captured Lin Chung three dances later

and said quietly, 'Dance us into the little parlour. I am very curious about Cynthia Medenham and the Major.'

'Her attentions to him have been marked,' he agreed, moving the pair of them towards the door and turning so that Phryne could see over his shoulder into the half-dark. The strange couple were still there, clasped close together. Miss Medenham was crushed in a strong embrace, and the Major was evidently much attracted. He lifted his head as Phryne and Lin Chung appeared, and glared.

Phryne smiled seraphically and nudged her partner back into the parlour. 'Interesting,' she commented.

'Phryne, are you really going to seduce that boy?' asked Lin Chung, sounding slightly offended.

'Possibly. I am wondering why he is making such a dead-set siege of me,' she replied.

'One can carry investigation too far,' he commented, avoiding Mrs Reynolds and the Doctor, who were deep in conversation, and swinging Phryne around the protruding edge of a large table against the wall.

'Not if one seeks the truth,' she said sententiously, and Lin Chung snorted.

'Come, come, my Confucian. If it were not for your exaggerated sense of ethics I would be sleeping with you,' she said. 'One must suffer for one's beliefs.'

'You,' said Lin Chung admiringly, surveying the

dark head with the panache of feathers, 'are a woman who could corrupt a monk.'

'So I would, if he were a pretty monk who didn't really think about his vows when he made them.'

Lin laughed.

Golden hair said to dark hair, 'It's no use. I'll never be free.'

'Yes you will,' said dark hair to golden. 'I'll make you free.'

'Kiss me again.' There was a sound of mouths meeting, frantically, and hands slid under a white shirt and dark coat to find skin damp with desire.

Golden hair broke away from the embrace with a groan. 'It's immoral, it's improper, we can't do this. What would people say?'

'Who cares what people say?' asked dark hair flatly. 'My love, my own love. Say it.' They kissed again. 'Say it, I want to hear the words.'

'My ... love,' faltered golden hair. 'My dear love, my own.'

The party wound down. Phryne found herself sitting next to the poet, looking through the family photograph albums.

'The Edwardian Indian summer,' he said in his accented voice. 'Here is the whole house party. By the rabbits I deduce that they have been hunting.'

'Gosh, Hinchcliff hasn't changed, has he? Or his wife. And there's Tom, looking every inch the

Lord of the Manor, and Evelyn, she looks so young, and who's that?'

'Her son,' said Tadeusz. 'Young Ronald. He went, as they say, to the bad.'

'Not Tom's child, then?'

'No. She had another husband. He died. She doted on that boy – doted on him, and that is very bad for the young.' Phryne stared at Mrs Reynolds' face in the fading sepia. She looked soft and happy and vulnerable, holding the hand of a tall young man with her sharp features and strong bones.

'I believe that he stole money from Tom – Tom forgave him, but then he stole from his employer and went to prison for two years. I remember him, this Ronald. He was sure of his worth, sure that he had *droit de seigneur* over the housemaids – Mrs Reynolds put him straight on that fast enough. The world owed him a living, like the grasshopper in the Aesop fable. He did not want to work but he was not prepared to forgo the good things – so he stole. A common tale,' said the poet, looking sad.

'What happened to him?'

'He ran away to America, I believe, where he worked on a cattle ranch. He wrote, for some little time, to his mother – always asking for money. She cried lamentably over those letters. Then – nothing. I believe that he is dead, but his mother keeps hoping. Poor Evelyn. A tragedy,' said the poet.

'So it is,' said Phryne, turning the pages. ' "She'd

have been different if the boy had turned out well." That's what Tom said at dinner.'

'So she might. I am worried about Tom Reynolds, Miss Fisher.'

'Me, too. I've never seen him that drunk. Who gave him that much juice?'

'I don't know. It was not me. A glass of this and a glass of that, even several bottles of that and this – I will indulge, happily. But sodden drunk at my wife's dinner party, no. I have never known him to display such bad form.'

'He's worried about Lina.'

'So am I. She is a nice girl, if a little fantastical, but that is no excuse for Tom to drink himself into social disgrace.'

'No. I do not like this house party, Tadeusz, and I wish I could get away.'

'I do not like this party either, Phryne, and I cannot write poetry in this atmosphere.'

'There are consolations,' she replied, and the poet grinned wickedly.

'There are, but mine appears to have taken up with another.'

'Mine has developed a deep concern for my reputation,' she confessed, and Tadeusz laughed and clasped her hand.

'There are others,' he chuckled, and Phryne smiled and patted his cheek.

'Jack and Gerald have been coming here for a long time,' she said, turning another page of the large leather-bound volume.

'Yes. There is old Mr Lucas – Jack's father. That

falling-out – it was a pity. They were such old friends. Yet it was not really Tom's fault. And there,' the broad finger stabbed at the page, 'that is the tramp, the one they are all scared of. Harry.'

'Dingo Harry?' Phryne peered at the picture. A stocky man in a collarless shirt and stockman's moleskins held up a long string of what must be dingo scalps. He was wearing a shapeless hat and grinning into the camera. His face was concentrated and intelligent, as far as one could tell through the mane of uncut hair and forest of beard.

'He is interesting; an educated man. When he wants to talk, which is seldom, he is worth the listening. I had a long conversation with him about the fall of the Paris Commune once, sitting on a rock in his little camp. Now there is a man who needs no material possessions. He is, regrettably, quite mad, but a poet should talk to the insane. Is not insanity just another way of looking at the world?'

'I suppose it is. Is he dangerous?'

'He has rages,' admitted Tadeusz. 'I have seen him seize a great branch and beat the walls of the cave with it, bellowing about the voices. Once I saw Evelyn tend him when he had beaten his head against a stone to let out the demons. But in between he is perfectly civilised.'

'Oh, good,' said Phryne, hoping that, if she met this character, he would be in one of his tolerant moods. 'Where is his camp?'

'Down by the caves. I fear, in fact, that he might

be flooded out by this storm. Is it still raining?'

Phryne listened beneath the music and heard the relentless swish of falling water. She nodded.

'Tomorrow we go to the caves; they are miraculous. Almost they could make me believe that a Divine Spirit and not chance ruled the cosmos. Almost. You are going?'

Phryne rose and smoothed down the jade velvet. 'Yes, I think I'll go to bed,' she said. 'Thank you for showing me the pictures. Good night, Tadeusz.'

He kissed her hand with a continental flourish.

Phryne found her hostess and bade her good night, waved a hand to the rest of the company and turned at the door. Lin Chung bowed a little from the chess table, where the Doctor had just made the first move. Gerald smiled at her, a breathtaking, glittering smile. The Major and Miss Medenham were still missing, presumably in the little parlour. Miss Mead smiled, a rather meaning smile.

Phryne climbed the monumental staircase, blew a kiss to the lady and the knight in the Morris windows, and came to her own room.

She tapped softly and called, 'It's me, Dot.'

There was a scraping as the chair was pulled away and Phryne slipped inside.

Dot had dined well, accepted one glass of light white wine, and was unaccustomedly flushed and pleased. Phryne dropped into a chair, pulled off the silver shoes and rolled down her stockings. Wiping the cold cream off her face with a cotton-wool swab, she asked, 'What's happened, Dot? You look excited.'

'Miss, you remember all that paper we took out of Lina's books? And her little box? I've been looking at it.'

'Good. What have you found?' Phryne slicked her face over with milk of roses, dried it and followed Dot into her own room, where she surveyed neat little piles laid out on the single bed.

'These are just chocolate wrappers and bus tickets and things, Miss, nothing written on them. But I've found some letters and this.'

Dot showed Phryne a diamond ring. The silver mounting was discoloured from having lain in the brass box, but the stone twinkled as bright as ice.

'That's a good diamond – a couple of carats at least,' commented Phryne. 'Where would a housemaid get fifty quid's worth of jewellery, do you think?'

'I don't know, Miss. And there's a letter.'

Phryne scanned it. It was written in an educated, flowing hand, in very black ink on cream-laid vellum. *Lina, I'll never forget you, R.* 'Hmm. No date, of course, or address, or anything betraying like that.'

'And this,' Dot produced her most important find. It was a torn sheet of typing paper lettered with black capitals. LINA, COME TO OUR OLD PLACE, R.

'Cryptic, but it might explain why she was out in the mist that night. And I've an idea who R is, too. Dot, well done. A pretty piece of sorting. Can you clean up that ring?'

'What are you going to do, Miss?' asked Dot, alarmed.

'I'll wear it and see who notices,' said Phryne. 'Tomorrow, when we go to the caves. You're a genius, Dot. This ridiculous, horrible case is beginning to make sense, I think. File all that stuff away. Keep everything, even the bus tickets, and we might get a breakthrough. Now, I've got a player in this odd masque coming to see me tonight. He'll be here soon. Lock your door and don't come out.'

'What if he's dangerous?' demanded Dot suspiciously.

'Then I shall scream and you can bean him with the poker,' said Phryne.

Dot did as she was bid, and Phryne put out all the lights but her reading light, stripped off the jade dress and donned her chrysanthemum robe, and sat down. There was a book on the dressing table and she opened it.

That the bones of Theseus should be seen again in Athens was not beyond conjecture and hopeful expectation: but thefe should arife so opportunely to ferve yourfelf was an hit of fate, and honour beyond prediction ... But thefe are sad and sepulchral pitchers, which have no joyfull voices; silently expreffing old mortality, the ruine of forgotten times, and can only speake with life, how long in this corruptibile frame some partes may be uncorrupted; yet able to outlaft bones long unborn and noblest pile amongft us.

She shivered. The house was silent. She closed the book and laid it down, next to a small stone urn which had, by some chance, appeared in her room.

As Phryne stared at this intimation of mortality, Gerald whispered at the half-open door, 'Can I come in?'

Phryne admitted him and then closed the door, jamming the Sheridan chair back under the handle. He watched this with some amusement.

'Are you expecting an enraged husband?' he asked.

'In this house an enraged elephant is quite possible. Well, dear boy, this is what you wanted – an assignation.'

He came towards her, the shirt front gleaming in the soft light.

'Oh, yes,' he whispered, touching her cheek. 'That is what I wanted. Most beautiful Phryne.'

He drew her down to sit on her bed and the slim hands dropped to the belt of the chrysanthemum robe. He had clearly had some practice at extracting a lady from her clothes.

She undid the soft shirt, noting that he had changed his clothes so as to be easier to undress, which, she thought, demonstrated experience. He smelt of Floris woodbine scent as the soft mouth kissed down from her lips to her throat and thence to the bared breast.

As Phryne allowed the robe to fall away and embraced Gerald's waist as he stood to remove the rest of his clothes, she had a vision straight from the learned Sir Thomas: she and her lover as dry skeletons lying together, pelvic bone to pelvic bone, bare tibia and fibia crossing as grinning skull kissed grinning skull in the coffined embrace of the long dead.

Perhaps Lin Chung was right. The presence of death was an aphrodisiac. Gerald, naked, threw himself into her arms, his hands light on her skin, his mouth urgent, demanding. She tasted something like desperation in his kiss.

She wrapped her thighs around his waist, clutching the curly head to her breast. Opposed to death there was always life.

The living skeletons melded together, hard flesh sinking into yielding flesh, and the young man gasped aloud.

'Oh, Phryne,' he sighed, lying next to her with his head in the curve of her shoulder.

'Gerald, my dear,' she said absently. The vision of the bones had not reappeared, and her body was satisfied and slumping towards sleep.

'You're so beautiful.' He ran a soft hand down the curve of her breast to her hip, cupping the bone.

'So are you,' she replied, stroking the curly hair, her hand resting on the entrancing delicacy of his nape. He was a boy, too young, perhaps, even to shave.

'I'd better go, though I'd love to stay with you all night.'

'Hmm,' she murmured.

'You will help me, won't you?' he asked, kissing her shoulder.

'Of course. Help you with what?'

'Jack, of course. My chum. I mean, I might have to marry Miss Fletcher, but I can't do that until he's settled.'

'You might *have* to marry – Gerry, have you seduced Judith Fletcher?' Phryne came awake with a rush. The young man sat up, the delicate cheek flushed, his skin slick with sweat and shining in the soft light, as beautiful as a Pre-Raphaelite angel.

'Why, would you mind?' he asked defensively.

'No, no, dear boy, but it seems unwise if you don't want to marry her,' she commented, wondering how on earth he had managed it with Mrs Fletcher watching her daughter's every move. 'I mean, is she really the person with whom you want to spend the rest of your life?'

'Well, no, perhaps not, but I have to marry, and she's in love with me.'

'That is not a good reason,' said Phryne severely. 'You don't have to marry yet – you've got time. Look at Letty Luttrell and the Major. She married in haste and the poor girl is repenting in sackcloth and ashes and has been for years. You might find it hard to get rid of a wife, Gerry, and in any case it's messy and expensive.'

'You don't know everything,' muttered Gerald.

'No, I don't,' agreed Phryne. 'Do you feel like telling me?'

Gerald shook his head and felt for his clothes. Phryne watched him dress, feeling a certain disappointment as the flannel bags slid up over the delicate loins.

She accompanied him to the door and he kissed her. She slid the chair away and looked into the corridor.

'No one. Good night, Gerry.'

He smiled his entrancing little-boy's smile and leaned his forehead, for a moment, on her shoulder. Then he was gone.

Phryne, suddenly awake, read three chapters of *Urne Buriall* before she could fall asleep.

CHAPTER NINE

For those two which are smooth, and of no beard, are
contrived to lie undermost, as without prominent
parts, and fit to be smoothly covered.

The Garden of Cyrus, Sir Thomas Browne, Chapter III.

In THE blackest dark, Phryne awoke.

Someone was trying her doorhandle. It had a
characteristic creak. Once, twice. Then the door
squeaked as someone pushed against it.

Phryne leapt out of bed, seized the poker, and
crept to the door. She could hear someone
breathing on the other side.

She slipped the chair out from under the handle
and pulled the door wide, poker raised.

She was confronted by a shocked young man
who jumped back three paces as a naked, heavily
armed and undeniably female fury occupied the
doorway. Her teeth were bared in a snarl and she
seemed perfectly capable of decapitating him with
one swipe of the iron rod she was flourishing.

'No, no, please.' He raised his hands.

'Jack Lucas, what are you about?' demanded Phryne, lowering the poker to shoulder level.

'I was looking ...' the young man blushed. 'I was looking for Gerry.'

'And he told you that he would be here?'

'No, no, I just guessed that ... I'm so sorry, Miss Fisher.'

He was staring at her. Her body was slim but muscular and with the raised weapon she looked like an *Art Décoratif* nymph lamp. Phryne was aware that she was naked but saw no reason to do anything about it. While she had her poker she was not in any danger from this utterly embarrassed young man.

'I think you'd better go back to bed, don't you?' she snapped.

'I'm sorry, I'm really sorry. Please forgive me ...' he said. Phryne did not reply and he made an awkward bow and hurried away.

Phryne shut the door, replaced the chair and went back to bed, laying the poker within easy reach on her pillow in case there were any more alarms in the night.

Phryne awoke as Dot placed her cup of tea on the bedside table.

'Dot, one thing must be done today, and I mean *must*,' she said, sipping the healing brew. 'Ask one of the housemen to find a nice big heavy iron bolt, the sort you put on gates, and watch him as he fits it to the inside of that door. I had two visitors last night, one invited and one very much uninvited. You'd think this was Flinders Street Station.'

'Yes, Miss. While he's about it he can fit one to my door, too. I don't feel safe here.'

'Neither do I. You can put this poker back with the fire irons, Dot, and find my Beretta. I want some bargaining power with the next intruder. By the way, Dot, did you put that urn on my dressing-table?'

'No, Miss, of course not.'

'Not only a bolt,' decided Phryne, 'but a new lock with a key as well. And find that gun, too. I'm going to have my bath.'

Dot, who did not approve of guns, laid out Phryne's clothes for a trip to the caves: black velvet trousers, handmade English hiking boots, a silk shirt and a loose woolly jumper knitted of many colours, with ducks and drakes across the front, before she rummaged for the little gun and the box of shells.

Phryne bathed in the bathroom down the hall, a shameless room with a Dutch water-closet on a dais like a throne, a bathtub big enough to wash a variety chorus, and blue and white willow-pattern tiles on the walls. The floor was of pink marble, chilly to the bare feet, but the water was plentiful and hot.

As her employer dressed, Dot removed the urn and returned it to its proper place. It belonged, she was told, in a niche in the great stair.

By the time she was descending the monumental staircase, Phryne felt human again. The memory of Gerald's mouth warmed her all through. A well-skilled young man, definitely worth the effort.

Breakfast was, as always, lavish. Several people were missing. Jack Lucas, Miss Fletcher, Mrs Luttrell and Gerald Randall, it appeared, were either breakfasting in decent privacy or had already been and gone. Tom Reynolds and the poet sat together at the big table. Tom looked rough. Phryne poured herself some tea and took a poached egg and some bacon, home-cured and delicious. Tom was staring at a piece of dry toast as though it was a personal enemy.

'The nasty effects of a hangover,' said Phryne judicially, 'are produced by dehydration. Isn't that right, Doctor Franklin?'

'Yes, indeed, Miss Fisher,' replied the Doctor. 'If I was prescribing for you, Tom, I'd order a gallon of barley water and bed-rest.'

'Bed-rest?' Tom barked a laugh which must have hurt his head. 'Can't rest. Can't sleep.'

'Then drink your tea, have another cup and a few sips of that nice lemonade which Mrs Croft has made for you, and I'll give you some pills for tonight that I guarantee will put an elephant to sleep,' said the Doctor. Tom did not precisely brighten, but he did not dull any further. He drank the tea and allowed the poet to refill his cup.

'How do we get to the caves?' asked Phryne. Tom blinked at her.

'We'll harness up the big dray. The track's all right that way. We just can't go back to the Bairnsdale road because it's still under water.'

Phryne needed to get Tom Reynolds alone, to tell him that Lina had gone out into the night to meet someone called R, but the poet, clearly concerned, was tending his hungover host like a mother.

Phryne sauntered out into the grounds alone to reconnoitre.

She was down by the boathouse when she heard splashing. Surely no one was swimming in that river. It was in spate. Phryne ran to the bank and saw a hand grasping for the remains of the launching ramp. She knelt, grabbed, and hauled with all her strength. Judith Fletcher's red face appeared, followed by the rest of her. She was considerably bruised and more wet than she had been since she'd been born.

'Gosh,' gasped the young woman, wiping her hair out of her eyes. 'Golly, that current's strong!' She staggered and sat down on the grass, as red as her swimming costume.

Phryne exclaimed, 'What possessed you to go swimming in that?' She indicated the torrent of grey water foaming past at the speed of a racing horse.

'There's a little sandy bay back there,' panted Miss Fletcher. 'Out of the tide. I thought it'd be safe, it looked calm enough. But the undercurrent snatched my feet out from under me and the next thing I knew I was drowning. I suppose I ought to thank you,' she added resentfully.

'It might be polite,' said Phryne.

'It wouldn't matter,' Miss Fletcher broke out

suddenly. 'It wouldn't matter if I was dead.'

'Wouldn't it?'

'I always say the wrong thing and Mother always disapproves of me and I'm sick of this. I'm wasting my life at house parties, trailed around like a slave on a chain to be bid for by bored boys.'

Phryne sat down on the bank and produced her cigarette case. Miss Fletcher had thrown herself face down on the grass and was tearing up handfuls of sedge with her fingers.

'Then why keep doing it?'

'I'm an heiress,' wailed Judith.

'Yes, so am I.' This shocked the girl enough to make her look up at the composed figure perched on the bank, smoking a gasper.

'You are? Why didn't they marry you to someone, then? Or did they?'

'They didn't because I refused to play. They can't make you marry, you know. They can't really do anything to you. I ran away to Paris when I was eighteen. How old are you?'

'Eighteen,' murmured Miss Fletcher. She sat up cross-legged on the green riverbank.

'Is it your money?'

'Yes, I suppose it is, though Mother takes a lot of it to run the house and buy me clothes and all that. The old man left it all to me.'

'Have you a trustee?'

'Yes. Nice old bird but Mother never lets me have him to myself.'

'What do you really want to do? Marry Gerry Randall? He's a nice boy.'

'Yes, he's nice. But I don't really know yet. He's dreamy, is Gerry, lazy. But very handsome.'

'Yes, very,' said Phryne, visited by a reminiscent vision of the naked young man with the curly hair.

'But what I'd really like to do is have a little farm somewhere and breed horses. I'd have my chums to visit and then I could shut the door on all of them, light my fire, sit down in my chair and listen to the silence.'

'Then what you need to do, my dear,' Phryne extended a hand and hauled Miss Fletcher to her feet, 'is go and see your nice trustee and tell him that's what you want to do. If he agrees, then all the mothers in the world won't be able to stop you. Tell him that you're tired of all these parties and if he doesn't comply with your wishes you'll marry a taxi-driver and fling all your worldly wealth away on gigolos. Tell your mother that, too. It might work. Has it occurred to you that she is actually living off your capital, and making your life a misery into the bargain? Now, get back to the house before you freeze, Miss Fletcher, and next time, think before you fling yourself into deep water.'

Judith Fletcher had the gaffed-cod look of soul's awakening on her round face. She goggled at Phryne for fully a minute before she lowered her head and ran for the house, whipped along by a chill breeze.

The boathouse would do, Phryne ascertained a moment later. And not only had it stopped raining, but the sun looked like it was trying to come out.

The stableman had the heavy dray out and was backing a stout horse into the shafts as she came past.

''Ere, 'old 'im,' he grunted, thrusting a leading rein into her hands. The piebald carthorse at the end of it was backing steadily away. He knew those shafts. At any moment they might spike him in the behind. They also meant that he would spend the next few hours dragging a heavy weight behind him instead of the leisurely day's grazing he had planned.

'Calm yourself,' said Phryne to the horse, looking it in the eye and keeping a steady pressure on the rein. 'No use kicking against the pricks, Dobbin dear. We all have our cart to drag and today you are for it.'

The horse, soothed by her voice, stepped a pace towards Phryne and allowed her to stroke his nose.

'Good on yer, Miss, now back 'im in 'ere.'

Phryne walked Dobbin around in a tight circle, then stood in front of him and laid a hand on his chest. 'Back, ho!' she said. 'Whoa back!'

Dobbin, uneasy, danced a little on hoofs the size of soup plates before stepping back between the shafts. Willis threaded the tug girths and Phryne caressed the fringed ears. Dobbin, once harnessed, appeared resigned to his fate. She handed over the rein to the ex-jockey and walked around the dray.

It was a huge, heavy, lumbering wagon, obviously designed for carrying tree trunks. It had been fitted with benches and could be covered with a canvas hood as seen in all the best westerns. Phryne half expected to hear someone play 'The William Tell Overture'.

She walked around the vehicle, noting its all-over muddiness and resolving to take an oilskin. Then she noticed a clean spot of bright metal in the centre of the front spoked wheel.

'Mr Willis, have a look at this,' she called, and the old man tutted, looped the rein over a mounting-block, and came to her side.

'Someone's been playing tricks again, Mr Willis,' she said. The axle nut was missing. Fresh sawdust on the muddy ground indicated that the axle itself might have been partially sawn through. Terry Willis rubbed a shaking hand over his gnome's face. He looked like a kobold who had just been told that he was mythical.

'Jeez, it'd take mebbe ten minutes to work loose, then ...'

'You know, I've lost all my taste for travelling,' commented Phryne. 'I think we'd better give Dobbin a holiday and tell the Boss that the trip to the caves is off.'

'Yair, reckon,' agreed the old man. 'You want to unharness 'im? I gotta get my boy and we gotta get this dray back inta the shed. Don't want every man and his dog ta know.'

Phryne found that unharnessing the carthorse was a lot easier than harnessing him. One just undid every buckle in sight and led the beast forward with his enthusiastic cooperation.

'There you are,' she hauled on the rein to bring

the big head down low enough so that she could take the headstall off past his ears. 'And a nice little walk back to your paddock. At least I've improved your day,' she said to the horse, who shook his head at the contrariness of humans and trotted back to his paddock, waited for her to unlatch the gate, and plodded through.

Tom Reynolds was as astonished as a man with a newly recovered hangover could be when he heard Phryne's news. Stopping only to pull on some gumboots, he rushed out of the house to interview Willis. The house party scattered in search of other diversions and Phryne went up to her room.

'I'm going for a walk, Dot,' she yelled to her maid, over the hammer blows of Mr Black, the houseman, who was fitting the bolt. Dot nodded. Phryne pulled on a heavy velvet-lined cape and went to find Lin Chung.

He was standing in the parlour, looking out of the window. When she came in, he asked quietly, 'How was the beautiful young man?'

'Beautiful,' said Phryne carelessly. 'But only beautiful.'

'And I?'

'Ah, you are quite different. Much more than just beautiful.'

Lin Chung sighed. Then he held out a closed hand to her. She opened his fingers and revealed a chess-piece. It was the Red King.

Phryne scanned the board, caught up a small

figure and laid the White Queen beside the Red King. The alchemical marriage. The Shanghai ring gleamed on her hand, next to a bright, silver-mounted diamond. Lin Chung took up their intertwined hands and kissed her palm.

Phryne did not care for hunting. Her view was that she had never been personally threatened by a rabbit (unless you took into account a villainous long-dead *lapin ragout* once served to her by a Marseilles cook of few morals and a penny-pinching disposition), so she saw no need to shoot them. She had sacked the cook, so that took care of him. And the rabbits, she considered, had enough problems without her persecuting them as well.

Wandering out into the grounds, however, she noticed Jack and the angelic Gerald heading out bush with a couple of rifles, apparently intent on slaughtering some of the local wildlife. That disposed of them. According to her careful investigations, the staff were all safely in the house. Tom was in the stables, Mrs Reynolds was arguing with the cook about bottled beans, the Major was apparently still sleeping off his dissipated evening and his wife was sitting on a bench under the beech tree embroidering. Miss Fletcher and Mrs Fletcher were playing the Victrola in the parlour and Miss Cynthia was inducing the Doctor to dance a foxtrot with her. The poet, having been inspired by the sight of Cave House at dawn, absurd amongst the gum trees, was in the library, immersed in ink and swearing under his breath in some Finno-Ugric language. Miss Mead was knitting in the parlour and Miss Cray was in the kitchen, attempting to extract contributions from the staff in aid of missions to the heathen.

The heathens Phryne and Lin Chung were drifting across the lawn toward the boathouse, which had a door that latched, a punt, two boats loaded with cushions, and the requisite amount of privacy.

Phryne found that she was breathing as if she had been running. They slipped inside, into a scent of old mattresses and varnish. The door had barely closed before she was unfastening the buttons of Lin's shirt, and he had pulled her jumper over her head.

'We can lie there, in the punt,' she said, as her shirt peeled away and his mouth came down to her breast. His silk shirt fell open and she wrapped her bare arms around his waist, his skin smooth and warm.

'And if we are surprised?' he breathed into her neck.

She laughed and said, 'We glare.'

They lay together in the boat, squeezed close in the semi-dark, on musty cushions and Phryne's velvet cloak. She sneezed, chuckled and gasped as his clever mouth found the right place.

She felt his body react to her touch. Under her fingers the jade candle was lit. When she managed to manoeuvre into the right position, it was extinguished inside her and she stifled a cry.

The butterfly danced on the flower. Lin Chung

lifted one of her hands to cover his mouth. She felt his jaw clench. Muscles tightened and trembled in thigh and buttock. He was a golden man, a brazen statue. She clutched his shoulders and they were as hard as iron; then she felt his lips thin as his climax bloomed inside her and her bones were filled with honey.

For a while she thought she was seeing stars, then realised that small shafts of sunlight were shooting arrows through the holes in the boatyard roof.

There was a weight in her arms, a beautiful man. The air was redolent of female musk and his hay-scented skin and she leaned up to lick beads of sweat off his throat.

'Silver Lady,' his voice was husky and very low, 'you are full of wonders. I was wrong, I cannot bear to be without you. Let me come to your room tonight. I will not be seen.'

'Yes. Ah, Lin, don't move – let me feel you, so close.'

They lay coupled in the boat, dust settling on them, heavy with completion, not yet sated, kissing, endlessly kissing.

The door opened. Phryne and Lin Chung lay still. Phryne had chosen this boat because it could not be seen from the door. And if she was going to be caught, she was not going to make an undignified, shamefaced scramble of the discovery. She would be found lying with her lover, and she hoped the finder would appreciate his truly remarkable beauty and her own.

The footsteps came closer – two people. They

heard the sound of a kiss on a long, gasping breath. Someone else, it seemed, had noticed the advantages of the boathouse.

Phryne, moving silently and with great care, edged around so she could see over the gunwhale. The other punt creaked as a young man unloaded the padding and spread it on the floor. He was evidently preparing a bed, and would be making love in Phryne's plain view. She heard a whisper. 'No, we can't.'

'Yes,' urged an unmistakably male voice. 'You know you love me.' Phryne heard the sound of something heavy and metallic being put down with a clatter.

'I love you,' agreed the whisper. Lin Chung had also moved; he was kneeling behind Phryne, his belly against her buttocks, both hands on her breasts. His touch, as always, sent sparks through her.

'I love you,' declared the whisper, louder this time. Phryne watched as a male chest was bared by skilled hands, to be mouthed and kissed by . . .

Another man.

Phryne had never seen men make love to each other. She would not have sought out the sight – available for a fee in certain places in Paris, for instance – but she could not move without alerting the lovers, and they were fascinating.

Beautiful. Gently, carefully, Jack peeled off Gerald's clothes, baring the slight body with olive skin, long thighs and the scribble of pubic hair. Gerald's dark curly head was drooping as his body relaxed into desire. Jack tore off his own clothes;

taller and paler than his lover, and dropped to his knees. He kissed and gently stroked the beloved body, then finally drew Gerald down onto the punt cushions. They kissed, first tentatively, unpractised, then with ferocious passion, locked mouth to mouth, chest to chest, thigh to thigh. They panted, grappled again, the dark arms around the pale back, the blond head sliding down to suckle. Finally they settled, then plunged together with bone-breaking force.

A jolt ran through Phryne at the strangeness and violence of their embrace. She reached behind her and Lin Chung responded, sliding forward until they were joined then moving gently, all noise covered by the ragged breath of the lovers, who drove together as though frantically trying to be one flesh in truth; Hermaphroditus, one body.

They were too passionate to endure long. As Phryne heard Lin Chung catch his breath and say her name in Chinese, as she sank under her own orgasm, she heard the young men cry out together.

Jack was lying on his back with Gerald's head on his chest as Phryne and her lover found ways to lie more comfortably in their punt. Phryne's skin was glowing with heat. She felt light-headed with relief and determined to not sleep alone in Cave House again.

Then, in the gloom, she heard Gerald begin to cry.

'There, Gerry, there . . . my . . . love, my love,' soothed Jack, stroking the dark hair.

'It's no good,' sobbed Gerald. 'We'll never be together – never. We're monsters, Jack. You'll never love women at all. I'll never love them like I love you, want you. We'll never be normal, they call us pansies – inverts. Oh, Jack, I do love you so.' He kissed Jack on the shoulder.

'Hush, love, hush. There will be a way. You're not ... you're not sorry that you're mine, that we ...'

'I'm not sorry.' Gerald kissed Jack again. 'You love me, I love you. It was bound to happen ... Jack, I've been thinking about you all night.'

'Not all night you haven't. I came looking for you.'

'Where?'

'Miss Fisher. She nearly beaned me with a poker.'

'You went to her room? Golly, Jack, what did you say?'

'Nothing much. She was beautiful, though. Looks like a Deco nymph with a snarl on her like Nike herself. I can see why you wanted her. Was it better, making love to a woman?'

'No. Of course not. Different. Lovely. But not this, not love. I had to try, Jack, you can see that. I had to see if ... she could help us, and she wanted me.'

'If you were a woman, Gerry, you'd be a tart.'

'Probably. I'd do anything – anything at all to have you, Jack.' They kissed again. Gerry faltered, 'Could you ... could you come to me? We can make it look like we sat up drinking and playing cards. No one will know. Come and ... sleep with me? I ... can't bear to lose you.'

'I'll come,' said Jack tenderly. 'We'd better go,

Gerry. We've been away a long time and not a single rabbit to show for it.'

'I suppose so.' Reluctantly, they found their clothes and dressed. Then they suddenly clasped together in a kiss which took Phryne's breath.

'But the hunting was good?' asked Gerry.

'The hunting was good,' agreed Jack.

The boathouse door swung to behind them.

'We'd better go, too, before someone else comes in to couple in the boathouse. I never saw such a place for assignations, and we're going to have to re-calculate our equation. They have a really good reason for wanting Tom dead. Which is a pity because I have a whole new bundle of news which I must tell you.' Phryne found her clothes and pulled them on, then searched for Lin Chung's shirt. As he buttoned it, she said, 'Watching them was arousing. They were so fierce. Did you feel it too?'

'A forbidden passion, once indulged, is like a forest fire,' he quoted slowly. 'They must have been desiring each other for years. It is a shame that their wedding had to be celebrated in a dusty place such as this.' He brushed a cobweb from Phryne's hair. She kissed a smear from his perfect cheek.

'You'll come tonight,' she said confidently.

'Yes, Silver Lady. I'll come!'

Half an hour later, Lin Chung was grave. 'So there was a son of the house who went to the bad. And there are the letters and the ring in the girl's pos-session. But who keeps leaving urns all over the place and what is their significance? Who wrote the notes to Reynolds and who sawed through the axle and laid that trap which almost killed you? Who killed Lina and why, and where is her body? And why should anyone take it? An uncomfortable possession, I would have thought.'

'The body was taken to conceal the death,' said Phryne. 'No body, no enquiries about where everyone was. I've just had a thought, Lin. I was told that the Major and Tom went out to fish yesterday, and we had trout last night at dinner. Oh, Lord, that dinner.' She broke off to laugh. 'Tom said he didn't catch any. I wonder if he was with the Major? That's the time we are looking at.'

'We can ask him,' said Lin Chung. 'I can hear him in the stables.'

The master's voice was indeed audible at forty paces.

'What do you mean, you didn't lock it?' he was bellowing.

'Listen, Boss,' returned Terry Willis with spirit. 'You never told me to lock the flamin' doors. Oo's gonna 'alf-inch a dray that size out 'ere? 'E'd need to steal an 'orse as well and we got the dogs. They raise the dead if so much as a fox comes past.'

'I reckon you're right,' said Tom, as Lin and Phryne came into the large, hay-scented shed. 'Shouldn't have lost my temper like that, old man.'

'Right then. You want the flamin' cart repaired?' demanded Willis, not entirely mollified.

'Yes,' said Tom heavily.

'Then you get onter Paul to make us a new axle, Boss. Iron one, this time.'

'Right,' said Tom, and Lin Chung and Phryne accompanied him out of the stable.

'We have a question,' said Phryne, laying a hand on his arm. 'Tom dear, I know you weren't yourself last night but you said you hadn't caught any fish. Did the Major catch any?'

'I don't know,' said Reynolds, patting her hand. 'You behaved very well at dinner, my dear Phryne, my dear Lin. I might have made a complete idiot out of myself, instead of just embarrassing Evelyn. She's forgiven me. I owe you a debt.'

'It's nothing,' murmured Lin Chung, and was overridden by Phryne, who said quickly, 'You do owe us a debt. Pay it by giving that young man his money and let's be rid of the whole scandal. I feel some responsibility for Megatherium, Tom. I knew the man who did it, and I didn't hand him over to the cops. He's in South America and I hope it chokes him and he didn't have a bean left of all that money, but still. As a favour to me?'

'I can't, Phryne. I'd like to but I rashly swore I wouldn't give him a penny. I gave my word ... I can't climb down.'

'Very well. A curse on all stiff-necked men. I have another plan.' She leaned on his arm and explained. Both Lin Chung and Tom looked utterly mystified.

'But how will that set him up for life?' he asked. Phryne smiled.

'Do you agree?' she asked.

'Yes, if you say so, Phryne, all right, I agree. That will be the end of the Lucas matter? Really?' His eyes sought Lin Chung's, as the only other responsible male present, but the Chinese shrugged in negation. He didn't understand, either. 'And that discharges my debt?' Tom asked.

Phryne grinned. 'Nobly.'

'Shake,' offered Tom, and Phryne shook his hand.

'If you can get Jack to agree, that will be a weight off my mind,' he admitted. 'Now what was it you were asking me?'

'Did you catch any fish?' repeated Lin Chung, who was a logical thinker.

'No. It started to rain and I felt a bit rheumatic so I came back and left him to it. Remarkable if he caught anything, considering the turbid state of the water.'

'So there is no one to say where the Major was when Lina was killed.'

'Perhaps,' suggested Lin Chung, 'we ought to go and ask the Major.'

CHAPTER TEN

Though earth hath ingrossed the name, yet water has
proved the smartest grave.

Urn Burial, Sir Thomas Browne, Chapter I.

THE MAJOR was not in his room. The door was
open and the bed neatly made. Phryne looked
around. There was a silver-framed photo on the
bureau; a splendid uniform, hung with campaign
medals, with a recognisable Major William inside.
There was a large and muddy oil of a wobbly
church on the wall and a few small pastels of
flowers. She noticed that her hands were trembling
slightly and wondered why. Then she tracked
down the memory.

Lina's freshly made bed, her clean room. Doreen
had obviously just left.

Lin looked across at Phryne and she returned the
glance with interest.

'Tom, dear, I think we ought to find the

Major,' she said meaningly. 'He might be ...
hurt.' Reynolds shook his head.

'Phryne, you're exaggerating.'

'Do I usually exaggerate?' she asked tautly.

'No,' he decided. 'No, you don't. All right.' He
pressed the buzzer and Phryne filled in the interval
while Hinchcliff climbed the stair by drifting
around the room, picking up small things and
putting them down. The usual bric-a-brac, she
thought: a terracotta Infant Samuel at Prayer who
clearly suffered from hydrocephaly; a blue china
vase full of dried grasses; a small stained-glass box;
and a tall medieval angel carved from some heavy
dense wood. She picked it up. The wings met over
the haloed head, the hands were pressed together
in piety, but the figure was unusual. This angel
neither bent his head in prayer nor stared blankly
at the viewer radiating divine messages. The
carved mouth was curved in a smile, the head held
at a slight angle. It was a delightful work.

'Tom, where did you get this?' she asked.

'Oh, do you like it, Phryne darling? It's all yours.
Just put it out of sight, don't let m'wife see it – the
boy carved it. I thought I'd got rid of all his stuff.'

'What boy?'

'Her son Ronald. He had a mania for Gothic art,
used to play all manner of games, knights and sar-
acens, that sort of thing. Ah, Hinchcliff. Have you
seen the Major this morning?'

'No, Sir.' Mr Hinchcliff seemed to convey, with
perfect politeness, that this had improved his day.

'Find out where he is, there's a good chap. We're

a bit nervous today what with Lina and all.'

'Certainly, Sir.' Mr Hinchcliff left the room, bestowing on Phryne not an actual smile, but an approving look. That was a young woman with the right stuff, he seemed to be thinking, despite her eccentric choice of companions.

Lin Chung volunteered to go and check the billiard room and Phryne agreed to meet him there in an hour. Then, cradling the angel, she returned to her room to put it away, and found her door not only closed but apparently barred. She knocked.

'It's me, Dot.'

Something clunked, a key turned, and the door opened just enough to admit Phryne. She gave the carving to her maid who held it uncertainly.

'Here, shove this in the baggage. Well, Dot dear, we seem to have a profusion of locks.' Phryne looked at the doorframe, which now sported a very large and elaborate iron bolt which could have secured a crypt, and a modern box-lock which opened with a key.

'Do you feel safer now, Dot?' asked Phryne, concerned. Her maid looked pale and unhappy. The strong ochre of her woollen house-dress cast a yellowish light on her milky complexion and her long hair had been even more firmly braided than usual, a sure sign that Dot was perturbed.

'Yes, Miss, and it stays locked and bolted whenever we're inside.' Dot pronounced firmly.

'Fine with me,' Phryne said gently. 'As soon as the river goes down we can go home, Dot.'

'Why, Miss, have you solved the murder?'

'I think so. Now you'll be called down for lunch soon, won't you? I want you to find something out for me. You should be able to turn the conversation around.' Phryne told Dot what she wanted. The maid nodded.

'All right, Miss, that doesn't seem too difficult. I found out about Mr and Mrs Hinchcliff like you wanted. They worked in one of the gentlemen's clubs in Spring Street. Mrs H says they were very happy there. She did the housekeeping and he was the butler. He's an imposing man, don't you think, Miss? Mr Reynolds used to come to the club, and when he married Mrs Reynolds he asked them to come with him. They had a son that died, Miss, and they wanted to get away, and Mr Reynolds pays them almost double what they'd get in the city, so they're saving up for their retirement. Mr Hinchcliff had a bit of a gambling problem, used to go to the races, but out here there's nothing to bet on. Except that he plays cards with Mr Black, Mr Willis and Mr Jones. They reckon he's an awful card player, but he can't lose money to 'em because Mrs H won't let them play for money. Mr Willis reckons he could build a new stable with the matches he's won from Mr H playing poker.'

'Well, well. The gambling bug has bitten Mr Hinchcliff, has it? Well done, Dot.'

'I'll go down to lunch, then. By the way, Miss, we've got another urn.'

'Oh, yes?' Phryne was struck with a sudden memory of Lin Chung like a flash of bright light. She blinked.

'Yes, Miss. It's on your dressing table. A nice white marble one.' Dot smiled. The situation had become less threatening now that there was a lot of secure ironmongery between her and midnight walkers. 'Oh, before I forget. There are two keys to our door, Miss. I've got one and here's yours.' Dot handed over a new silver key and went out, ostentatiously locking the door behind her.

Phryne put the key in her bag. Someone was either trying to scare her or help her by scattering urns in her path with such a liberal hand. If it was designed to frighten it hadn't worked. If it was someone trying to help her, she owed it due consideration. She sat down to examine the urn. It was, as Dot had said, made of white marble, and according to the worn gold lettering on the base it contained the mortal remains of someone called Mrs Claybody.

This was apposite, though Mrs Claybody was now ash rather than clay. Phryne took a sheet of paper and examined the lid.

It was fixed on with what looked like old sealing wax, which had been broken fairly recently. She breathed a half-serious apology to whatever might remain of Mrs Claybody and tipped the contents of the urn out onto the paper.

A small quantity of fine, grey, bonfire ash spilled across the paper. Phryne shook the urn and turned it upside down. There was nothing else inside. She poked through the ash with one finger, locating what might have been fragments of bone, but nothing unusual.

Phryne poured Mrs Claybody back into her last resting place and replaced the lid. The urn contained no clue. Assuming that someone in the house was trying to provide her with some direction, and not just indulging in diseased rural humour, the clue was not in the urn.

The clue must be the urn itself.

Phryne looked at it. Mrs Claybody had been provided with an elaborate container. The white well-polished marble had been carved by a good craftsman into a curvy, satisfying shape, and no expense had been spared in the matter of gilt lettering and gold handles. It was a period-piece of high Victoriana and Phryne hoped that Mrs Claybody, wherever she currently was, appreciated it.

Then she leapt to her feet as if stung. White marble, gilt, and curlicues. She had seen something like it in the house.

She unlocked and relocked the door with speed and walked quickly down the stairs to find Lin Chung.

He was in the billiard room, watching Jack Lucas angle a cannon. The spotted white ball bounced off an ivory ball, rolled and then kissed the red ball into a pocket. The watching poet applauded. Miss Medenham said, 'Oh, good shot!' Gerald complained, 'Jack, you are really too good at billiards to have had a virtuous youth.'

The double meaning of what he had just said struck the young man, and he bit his lip and blushed. Cynthia and Jack Lucas both laughed. Miss Mead, who had been looking at her crocheting, shot them a sharp look.

'Lin, dear, can I have a word?' said Phryne. He came with her into the alcove formed by the French windows. 'We've got to get into the cellar,' said Phryne, smiling indulgently on the lovers.

'Why?'

'Don't you remember? Oh, of course not, you weren't with me. There's a white marble sarcophagus down there, and someone has just left a white marble urn in my room. There's nothing inside it but what you would expect to find in an urn, so it must be the clue. Where's Tom? We need the cellar keys.'

'He's at the stables. Apparently the Major went riding this morning and has not returned.'

'Did he? I hope he hasn't met with an accident,' said Phryne concernedly. 'The horse might have been injured.'

'Phryne, what a wicked thing to say,' said Lin Chung, largely as a matter of form.

'Absolutely. Jack really is a good player, isn't he? I have to agree with Gerald's comment.'

The spotted white ball struck the green baize side of the table, flew across the surface, and the fated red ball dropped into a pocket again.

'Billiards is a game for gentlemen – a very Chinese game, really, positional. Of course, one cannot play snooker in a refined house like this,' commented Lin, and Phryne scanned his smooth face for irony. It was just not possible to guess what he was thinking from his expression. He exhibited all the blank solemnity of a stuffed fish, especially when delivering the most devastating barbs. It was an irritating trait. Equally, he was the object of Phryne's profound desire and the touch of his hand as he laid his fingertips gently on her shoulder made her shiver.

'Coming?' she asked, and he followed her from the room.

Hinchcliff surrendered the keys to Miss Fisher, detaching them from his watchchain. 'Mr Reynolds told me to render you all the assistance in my power, Miss Fisher.'

'Hinchcliff, are there other keys to the cellar?' asked Phryne.

'I believe there was another bunch, Miss, but they were lost years ago. Mr Reynolds left them in the garden somewhere.'

'I see. I'll be careful of the stairs,' she promised, as the warning rose to his lips.

The cellar was as dark as the inside of a whale. Phryne groped for and found the light-cord and pulled. They winced away from the glare of the naked bulb.

'There,' she said, pointing back into the dim recesses.

The floor of the cellar was slick and slippery, though someone had pumped out the standing water and re-capped the well. The marble object – surely it could not really be a sarcophagus, even in Cave House – stood solidly under a pile of tea-chests and crates.

'This looks as though it hasn't been touched for years,' said Lin Chung, observing a bloom of green slime along the white marble.

'I know, but I haven't got a lot to go on and that urn was left there by someone who wanted to tell me something. Wait a bit.' She lifted a crate of empty bottles and lay them aside on a stack of mildewing trunks. 'Look, Lin. The lid's been shifted. See that nice growth of algae? It follows the line of the lid. How do you feel about dead bodies?'

'I am not enamoured, but carry on.'

They cleared away the last of the impedimenta. Phryne picked up a case-opener, which bore a distinct resemblance to a jemmy, and inserted it under the lip of the tomb.

'I'll lever, you slide,' she said, holding her breath.

The lid resisted for a moment, glued fast with mould. Then Phryne managed to lift it enough for Lin to grasp the edge and pull it towards himself. It screeched as the worked edges scraped across each other.

Phryne and Lin bent to look inside.

At that moment, the light went out and cellar door clanged shut with a hollow boom.

Dark hair said to gold hair, 'It's happening.'

'What's happening?'

'The train of events that will bring us together – my love, my dear love.'

'What have you done?' said gold hair to dark hair, both hands on a serge-clad chest, resisting the embrace.

'I have done what I had to do.'

'For us?' asked gold hair.

'For us,' said dark hair tenderly and this time gold hair accepted the kiss.

'Phryne?' Lin asked. He let go of the stone lid, which balanced on the edge of the coffin. Phryne stretched out a hand, touched his hair, and slid down to grasp his wrist.

'Well, here we are,' she said excitedly. 'Someone doesn't want us to find out what is in this box. I must be getting somewhere. It's most gratifying.'

'Gratifying?' asked Lin Chung.

'Absolutely. Now, if you can come towards me, around the coffin, we should be about three paces from the stairs.' She moved slowly, sliding her feet across the slippery floor, anxious not to collide with anything. Her groping touch found a wall.

'Good. I've got a reference point.' Lin came to stand beside her. 'Now all we need to do is walk along this wall until we reach the stairs.'

'The door is locked,' Lin pointed out. 'Do you have the key?'

'Yes, of course. Or rather, no. I left it in the door, on the other side. Dammit. We're locked in. But at least we can have some light and there must be a way out of this cellar.'

'We will need to find it,' said Lin imperturbably out of the darkness.

'Oh, why?'

'Because the floor, dry enough when we came in, is now an inch deep in water. That well, as you recall, floods the cellar. If the water rises high enough . . .'

'It won't. Tom would never let his precious wines get wet. There, there are the stairs. Follow me up,' she said, as he placed his hand on her waist. They splashed through the cellar and up the castle stairs. Phryne counted. Five steps and a turn. Five more and another turn. Then she stood up with one hand on her guiding wall and flailed for the light cord. She caught at spider webs, but otherwise there was just empty air.

'Lin, I can't find the string for the light.'

'He could have brought it along the ceiling and jammed it in the door.'

'So he could. Further up. Here's the door. You take that side, I'll take this.'

They groped around the edges of the cellar door. It was a thick, solid wooden door, studded with iron nails with large heads. Phryne did not like their chances of chopping through it, even if they had a battleaxe. Though there might even be a battleaxe in the cellar of Cave House, probably along with a full set of fourteenth-century plate armour and the knight who wore it.

Lin said, 'There's no cord. He must have cut it.'

'Never mind. There's a little light; my eyes have got used to it now. Hinchcliff knows where we are. Someone will come and rescue us.'

'However, since it might take them a while to miss us, we might make some arrangements for our comfort,' he suggested.

He felt his way down the stairs again and Phryne heard him floundering in the dark, swearing in Cantonese, and splashing in what was evidently rising water.

He came up again and she felt him sit beside her on the broad top step.

'A bottle of wine,' he said, setting it down. 'Champagne, by the cork. I've also got the case-opener, which we might try on the door, and the cellarman's cushion for his port, when it was brought here in the dray. I fancy that it is an old bedcover. Are you cold?'

'Yes.' Phryne accepted half of the quilt, which stank of mould, and snuggled closer to Lin who was always warm. He bent to kiss her and she felt him shudder.

'Are you cold, too?'

'No. It's not the cold. I ... I don't like this place.'

'Neither do I,' she agreed.

'I mean,' he said with exquisite embarrassment, 'I do not like confined spaces and I especially do not like confined dark spaces.'

'I see. Well, no point in sitting here, then. Come on. Let's heave at that door.'

Lin found the lock and tried to force the claws of the case-opener into them. After a few minutes, he grunted, 'No good,' and gave the implement to Phryne.

'It's a well-made door,' she agreed after a moment's struggle. 'It's perfectly fitted and the lintel is of stone, curse it. It's no good, Lin dear, we shall just have to bang on the door until someone comes and lets us out. You can take first shift.'

Lin swung the iron bar against the unmoving portal and it clanged.

After about a minute, a partially deafened Phryne took the bottle and the quilt and removed herself to the bottom of the stairs. Her foot splashed down into water that was now at least ten inches deep and she withdrew two steps, suppressing her exclamation of disgust. The water was stagnant and foul with floating debris. She shook her wet foot like a cat who has put a paw into an unexpected puddle, squeezed water from her sock and trouser leg and dried her hands on her jumper.

Then she unwound the wires and popped the cork of the champagne, taking a deep gulp. Now was probably not the time to wonder aloud to her claustrophobic companion about what was actually in that sarcophagus.

The noise filled the cellar and echoed dully. After about ten minutes, Phryne called, 'Come down and have a drink, Lin. I don't think they can hear us.'

He laid down the bar and the noise stopped. Phryne swallowed and her hearing, in some measure, returned. She shared her musty cloak with him. He was panting with effort.

'It's embarrassing, Lin dear, not catastrophic,'

she said quietly. She felt him gasp a little as he gulped the rather good champagne – French, Phryne was sure, though not Veuve Cliquot – and he sat still and began to control his breathing. The heart which had been racing against her cheek slowed and firmed.

'I am forgetting my training,' he said into her hair. 'My master always said I was impetuous. "In the true way there is only calm", he said. I can hear him saying it.'

'Master?' asked Phryne encouragingly.

'Yes, Master Wu. I studied at the Temple of the War God in Peking. Only for a couple of years. Long enough to learn some discipline, I would have thought, but I have always been afraid of being locked in the dark. When I was a child I had a nurse who used to shut me in a cupboard if I displeased her. I'm ashamed, Silver Lady, to show such weakness.'

'It's nothing to be ashamed of. If you aren't afraid, you can't be brave.' She knew that this was insufficient and gave him something very close and secret. 'I'm afraid of fire.'

'Fire?'

'Yes. The pain of a burn hurts me more than anything else – the brassy taste in the mouth, that cold pain. If we were facing a fire, I'd be scared half to death, whereas a little cold, wet and confinement does not worry me unduly, though when I find whoever shut us in I'll do him an injury. Don't worry, Lin. I don't think any less of you. We're all afraid of something.'

'And you are a warrior,' mused Lin, pulling the quilt closer. 'Li Pen said so, and he would know, being one himself. He came out of that temple after ten years, Silver Lady, a complete fighter and hunter. That is why my father engaged him. He protects me, as well as irons my shirts and makes sure that I do not forget that I am Chinese.'

'Then he will be looking for you,' soothed Phryne.

'That is so.' Lin's voice was firm again. 'And he will find me. The trouble is, Silver Lady, that if we are missing together, people will make a certain deduction, and refrain from disturbing us.'

'Hmm.' Phryne's mind raced. If this was the case, they might be in the cellar until dinner time. By then the water, fed by the flooded river as well as the spring, might have risen to the ceiling, drowning even that marble coffin with who knew what inside it. She had a moment of sheer superstitious panic, let it flow over her, and drank some more wine. The bottle was perceptibly lighter when she commented, 'I wonder if there's another way out of this cellar?' She embraced Lin and stroked his cheek. He leaned his forehead on her shoulder, much as Gerald had done.

'There might be. This is the sort of place to have secret passages.'

'Yes, but one really needs light to find one. Let's see. There must be candles somewhere and I've got matches in my pocket, how foolish of me.'

She drew out the box very carefully and lit one. By its light, she scanned the cellar, sighting what she wanted on top of a wine rack in the far corner.

'Right. There's a box of candles over there and no reason why we should sit in the dark. How many matches do we have?'

'Fifteen.'

'Good. Come down and start striking.'

'How will you get across?' he asked as she headed toward the bottom of the stair.

'I'll wade.'

Phryne fought off a wave of revulsion and stepped down into the cold unclean water. She skirted the wall by the uncertain light of the match, knowing that somewhere in the middle was the well. The water was knee-deep now and freezing. Unseen objects rolled underfoot, threatening to fling her face down into the scum. She clung to the wine racks and reached the other side. There was a little light from a skylight of opaque glass barely a foot across.

There were eleven candles in the wooden box and a container of matches. She lit three tapers and instantly the dark was banished to lurk in the corners.

Across the expanse of black water she saw Lin Chung standing on the step shaking his burned fingers. She winced in sympathy.

'There we are. Light. Now, what do we need to look at?'

'The sarcophagus,' he said bravely. Phryne sloshed across to it, steeled herself, and peered in.

'Nothing, it's empty. Hang about,' she added,

bringing the candle closer. 'There's a bit of crumpled fabric here, some fluid of some sort, and, erk, rather an awful smell. I think she's been here, Lin, but she's not here now. That's a relief, eh? I'm going to have a look at the far wall. Back in a tick.'

'I'm coming, too.' Lin stepped down. Phryne smiled at him. In the flickering light, her eyes glowed as green as a cat's. She gave him a taper and put the piece of material from the coffin in his pocket.

'They never make women's clothes with enough pockets,' she complained, holding her candle high and clambering over crates and boxes.

'Perhaps so that gentlemen with pockets can feel useful,' said Lin, pushing aside what appeared to have been a wardrobe trunk for ocean travel before the sides had caved in.

'Now, we are under the servants' hall,' reasoned Phryne. 'This appears to be a boundary wall, what do you think?'

The weight of the house was pressing down on Lin Chung like a boulder on the back of his neck. He coughed, shook himself, and said, 'Yes, it's well built and it must be the outer surface of the house.'

'Good, now for the other ones. What do you think has happened to the Major?'

'I have no idea. He might have run away. Perhaps Miss Medenham and he could not agree and he rode off in a fit of pique. He might have fallen off his horse and not landed as lightly as you did, Silver Lady.'

'Aha,' said Phryne.

'Aha?'

'Come here, Lin, look at this stretch of wall. What's different about it?'

'It's brick,' he said. 'The other walls are stone.'

'It's brick and it's decorated,' she said, feeling along tuck-pointing and around white mortared borders. 'Look for the pattern which doesn't match the rest of the wall.'

'Here,' he said, puzzled, laying a palm on slimy bricks laid lengthwise and criss-crossing. 'This is the only part like this.'

'Good. Now pull, push and twiddle everything which looks twiddleable.'

Lin obeyed long enough for his candle to burn down. Phryne gave him another one.

'This is futile,' he protested. 'The water's rising. Hadn't we better go back up the stairs?'

'In a little while.' Phryne, the water almost at her hips, pounded a likely-looking brick, then leaned on a particularly careless obtrusion of mortar. Nothing happened and the water continued to rise.

'Dammit,' she muttered. 'You're right. Let's go back.'

He reached out to take her hand as she began to clamber over a fallen dresser which might have been designed for Alfred the Great. She slipped, slid, and fell against the wall, swearing in a variety of languages.

'*Dommage*,' she said as he hauled her to her feet. 'Now I'm wet through, and all for nothing. It was a silly idea, Lin.'

He did not answer. The bricks groaned. Lin dropped his candle and flung himself against a moving wall. A dark crack widened and then the door gave way.

Phryne, Lin Chung, and a thousand gallons of water spilled out of the cellar of Cave House into light.

CHAPTER ELEVEN

Darkness and light divide the course of time, and
oblivion shares with memory a great part of our
living beings; we slightly remember our felicities, and
the smartest strokes of affliction leave but short smart
upon us. Sense endureth no extremities, and sorrows
destroy us or themselves.

Urn Burial, Sir Thomas Browne, Chapter V.

IT WASN'T as bright as sunlight. Phryne hooked her
fingers over an iron projection and Lin Chung was
flung against her by the force of the water, almost
carrying them both along with the stream. He
grabbed another iron rung and Phryne spared one
hand to grasp at his shoulders, bringing her feet
up out of the water.

'A life on the rolling wave,' she commented. 'Are
you all right?'

'Wet but undamaged. How about you?'

'Wetter but also undamaged.' She released her
hold as the first rush of water drained away.
'Where are we? Some sort of tunnel?'

'Let's find out where it leads,' suggested Lin Chung. Phryne heard the steely control in his voice and led the way down a paved stone passage like a stormwater drain. The light was honest daylight. Twenty paces revealed that the opening was narrow, perhaps three feet wide. Phryne ducked to go under the lip and found herself in a small sandy bay, knee-deep in a fast-moving stream. She grabbed for Lin and warned, 'Look out! This must be the river!'

He climbed carefully up the bank and lifted Phryne out of the water, setting her down beside him. She felt him draw a huge breath of relief. She groped for her cigarettes and found, to her delight, that the case was waterproof. Lin lit their last match and she inhaled gratefully. She was wet through, slimy and mouldy, but unhurt, and her Chinese companion was revealed to be a brave man. That, she thought, was worth a ducking. The sun shone weakly in a pale-blue sky and Phryne was dazzled after so long in the dark. The air smelt delightfully of wet grass and horses.

'There's Cave House,' Lin said. 'There's the stables, and there's Mr Reynolds.'

'Phryne dear, what have you been doing?' asked Tom Reynolds, reigning on his hack, apparently much astonished by their appearance.

'I took a fancy for a little swim with all my clothes on,' she said tartly. 'Where are you going?'

'To look for the Major. I'm going back along the bridle path, Tadeusz is going along the road as far as he can, Miss Fletcher is taking Brindle along the riverbank, and Willis is covering the paddocks.'

'Fine. Go ahead.' Phryne waved the cigarette. Tom stared, then shrugged. Phryne and Lin Chung began their walk back to Cave House. The poet passed them on a thoroughbred, riding as easily as if he was sitting in an armchair, with a stock saddle and long stirrup-leathers. Something about his seat jogged Phryne's memory. She had seen someone riding that way before. A parade came back before her eyes. Men riding through Pall Mall, and hats loaded with waving emu feathers.

An hour later, much recovered, Phryne and Lin Chung watched Hinchcliff question the staff. The butler had been shocked by the danger into which the honoured guest had been put, and was adamant that he had not locked the door. He had checked the door on his usual rounds and, finding it locked and the keys gone, had assumed that Miss Fisher had concluded her visit and had carelessly taken his keys with her.

The combined anxiety of Dot and Li Pen had persuaded the household that something was wrong, and a search had revealed the cellar broken open and the prisoners gone. Li Pen and Dot had met the bedraggled adventurers as they dripped up the gravel path to the door.

Phryne had been bathed and scolded by Dot, Lin had been bathed and scolded by Li Pen, and both were feeling virtuous and comfortable.

'Now, I will know the meaning of this,' the Butler began portentously. 'The keys are here, they were left on the kitchen table. Who locked the cellar door?'

The maids exchanged glances and shook their heads. Doreen plucked up courage and said, 'It wasn't me, Mr H, or Annie. We was together with Mrs Croft in the kitchen, having a cuppa. I couldn't get into the room I was meant to be cleaning, because Miss Fisher's had a lock put on her door, and Annie couldn't do the billiard room while the gentlemen was playin'. So we came down here. We'll do the rooms later.'

Mr Hinchcliff looked at his wife – the housemaids were her province – and Mrs H nodded. Mrs Croft spoke up. 'And the skivvy was washing up the whole time – I could see her.'

'We 'aven't been in the 'ouse all day,' grumbled the gardener, and his boy muttered, 'Too right.'

'I was in the stables tryin' to fix that flamin' dray,' said Mr Willis, 'and me boys with me.'

'I was in the toolshed, looking for bits and pieces to finish that model for Alfred,' said Mr Jones. 'He was with me.' The boy spoke up, impelled by a poke from the toe of Mr Jones' shoe. ''Sright, Boss, we was.'

All eyes turned to the only remaining member of staff.

'It was me,' confessed the mechanic. Phryne looked at him properly for the first time. Mr Paul Black was a strongly built, thickset man; a contrast to the tall slim Jones. His face was scarred, so liberally smeared with grease that it was hard to guess his features, and his lank black hair was apparently styled with sump oil. 'I saw the door open and I couldn't see anyone inside. The light wasn't on, so I assumed that Mr H had forgotten to close it. The keys were in the lock. So I shut the door and locked it and left the keys on the table,' he said, in a whining tone which set Phryne's teeth on edge. She spoke coolly.

'Mr Black, the light was on. I have since ascertained that the string for the light has been cut. You must have known we were there.'

'I thought . . . you mighta wanted ta be alone,' he grinned, and Phryne fought down an urge to start throwing things. There was a fine heavy skillet to hand and she thought that Mr Black's looks could hardly be damaged further by a good solid metallic impact. And this would make Phryne feel much better.

'Then you knew we were there and you shut the door anyway?' asked Lin Chung relentlessly.

'It was a joke!' wailed Mr Black.

'A joke?' bellowed Mr Hinchcliff, filling up with air like a bloater fish. 'Out you go, my lad, and that today. Get your traps.'

'Hang on, you can't fire me!' protested Mr Black. 'I demand to see the Boss!'

'You can't, he's out hunting for the Major,' said Phryne. 'So you want to stay here, Mr Black?'

'Yes.' He hung his head, then knelt and pawed at Phryne's immaculate knee. 'Don't let 'im fire me, lady. I'm sorry. I didn't know the water came up that high. It was just a joke, lady. Please!'

Lin Chung removed the dirty hand and Phryne stood up.

'We shall see, Mr Black,' she said. 'Turn out your pockets, please.'

'Eh?' He gaped at her, still on his knees.

'Your pockets, Mr Black,' she insisted. Li Pen held Mr Black terribly still in some oriental hold while Lin and Mr Hinchcliff searched him.

'Interesting,' said Phryne. There was the string from the light, neatly rolled into a little bundle. There were seven shillings and threepence, a spark plug – she had never known a mechanic who did not have at least one spark plug on his person, it was a badge of office – a clasp knife, an indelible pencil, and a bunch of keys. Mr Hinchcliff pounced on them and exclaimed, 'Mr Reynolds' lost keys!'

'Let's see, what else? A few wood shavings, a box of matches, a packet of Woodbines, nothing else of consequence. Let him go, Li Pen, if you please,' said Phryne very politely. Li Pen was holding a man twice his own weight helpless in an effortless and efficient manner. She was always likely to respect anyone who could do that.

Li Pen released Mr Black and he scooped his belongings back into his pockets, shaking with outrage.

'There now. You shall see the Boss when he comes back from his ride. But I'd spend the time packing and paying off any small debts, if I were you. I know that the road to Bairnsdale is cut, but you can get to the township of Buchan from here, cross country, and the walk might do you good,' commented Phryne.

Mr Black snarled, showing broken teeth. For a moment it seemed that he might attack this smooth, insolent woman, and Phryne saw a smile of pure anticipatory happiness cross Li Pen's bronze face.

Then Mr Black spun around and threw himself out of the kitchen. Phryne and Lin Chung withdrew, hearing Mrs Croft say savagely behind them, 'Good riddance to bad rubbish. Now, I'll just put the kettle on, and we'll all feel better for a nice cuppa tea.'

'Was it a joke?' asked Lin. 'If so, I fear that I will never really understand Western humour.'

'It wasn't a joke,' Phryne assured him soberly. 'Now we know where the man in boots went with Lina's body. Li Pen lost him by the riverbank. He just walked to that little bay, went in through the tunnel and laid the body in the sarcophagus. Doreen says that the bit of material is from Lina's nightdress. Mrs Reynolds gives her old clothes to the staff, and Lina bagged a rather good pale-blue silk negligee, over Doreen's spirited bidding, apparently, which is why the girl remembers it. The body was there.'

'Then where is it now?'

'Best place to put it would be the river, now it's running so strongly.'

'Yes, but wait a bit – why didn't he throw the body into the river in the first instance? He had no need to go to all that trouble,' protested Lin Chung.

'Perhaps he wanted to keep her.'

'What on earth for? You are chilling my blood, you know.'

'Nonsense. Your blood doesn't chill that easily, my dear.' Phryne smiled up into his face. 'Who can fathom why murderers do things? Perhaps she reminded him of his mother. Perhaps she still held some attraction for him – what a revolting thought. Come on, I'm hungry, let's see if we can get something to eat.'

The riders returned mid-afternoon, just in time for afternoon tea. Phryne, who had not lunched and had only been able to prevail on Mrs Croft for a sandwich, was ravenous, and sat herself in front of a table laden with more sandwiches, three kinds of cake, and bread and butter. She was joined by the poet and Miss Cray, both possessed of healthy appetites.

The bread was homemade and the butter home-churned, the sandwiches well filled and the cake excellent, and it was some time before Phryne remembered her manners. Guests must carry on light conversation at afternoon tea, not sit there wolfing down the provender as though they had not eaten for months.

'Tell me about your work, Miss Cray,' she said,

a safe gambit in ordinary circumstances. The crabbed woman swallowed a mouthful of bread and said, 'The heathen, Miss Fisher. I am determined that they will be brought to see the light.'

'Oh, which heathen are we talking about?' asked Phryne, intercepting a glance from Lin Chung and suppressing a smile.

'All of them,' snapped the woman. Phryne leaned closer, fighting off her distaste for Miss Cray's scent. Holy poverty, it seemed, did not allow for luxuries like clean clothes. She smelt like a ragbag which had been left out in the rain and her nails were apparently in mourning for the state of the Faith.

'That's a tall order, Miss Cray. What church are you working for?'

'The Christian Church.' Miss Cray seemed uncomfortable. 'I can expect your donation soon?'

'Yes, I'll write you a cheque this very afternoon. To whom should I make it out?' Phryne's curiosity was piqued.

'To me. I will distribute it where there is need. For there is great need, Miss Fisher. The people walk in darkness all over the world – in the South Sea Islands, in China, in the heart of Africa. There are millions who have never heard the Word. China particularly,' said Miss Cray, fixing Lin Chung with a glittering eye, then remembering Phryne's promise and restraining her missionary zeal.

'The people who walk in darkness have seen a great light,' murmured Miss Mead. 'This is a great work, Miss Cray. One is reminded of the Acts of the Apostles.'

'Indeed,' muttered Miss Cray, putting down her plate. She seemed to have lost her appetite. She bundled her weeds together and stood up.

'I go to pray for the world,' she announced, and went.

For some reason, Miss Mead smothered a small smile, and a monstrous idea bloomed in Phryne's breast. She dismissed it instantly. Impossible.

'Tell me, Miss Mead, what do you do?'

'Nothing much, Miss Fisher. I live in a small house in the city, and it is such a treat to be out here in the country, in such a well-run household, too.'

'Tell me, Miss Mead, do you have a theory about the disappearances of Lina and the Major? Do you think they are connected?'

'Oh yes, dear. Sure to be. Strange the world may be, but not, I think, so strange that first a maid and then a guest vanish independently.'

'My feeling also,' murmured Phryne, taking up the plate of lemon cake and offering it to Miss Mead. The old woman's blue eyes were very sharp and perceptive, but Phryne had nothing to hide and felt no threat.

'Do you think that the unhappy maid is dead, Miss Fisher?'

'I do, Miss Mead. Though I am not sure about the Major. In both cases there were few clues – the rooms had been cleaned.'

'It is, as I said, a well-run house. Perhaps – I am

loath to suggest something which you must have thought of yourself, Miss Fisher – but perhaps the only two people who might know where the Major was going are Miss Medenham and Mrs Luttrell.'

'Yes, I had thought of that, and I shall get around to them in time.'

'Of course. Have you seen many plays this year, Miss Fisher? I went to *Ruddigore*, and it was very charming entertainment. The singing, particularly, was very fine.'

'Yes, very fine. Have some cake,' said Phryne.

On the other side of the room, the poet and Tom Reynolds were discussing the search. Lin Chung drifted closer.

'We've covered all the places he could have gone. It must be the caves, Tadeusz. Miss Fielding found the bay straying near the road to Buchan. The river's cut the road to Bairnsdale and it's the only way he could have gone.'

'It could be the town,' objected the poet. 'Perhaps he's sick of our company and wanted the bright lights.'

'Tadeusz, you know that Buchan hasn't got any bright lights. The Major could have dropped in at the Coffee Palace for a cuppa but that's the extent of the place.'

'Well, perhaps he doesn't like your coffee. It is truly awful, you know.'

'Don't know, never drink the stuff. Why don't

you go and tell Mrs Croft that her coffee is terrible?'

'Because, Tom, I have never liked being hit with pots. Listen. His wife says that he didn't come to bed last night – not with her, anyway. So he must have been elsewhere. Willis says that the horse was missing when he got up. It must have been someone the dogs know or there would have been a noise.'

'Tadeusz, how do'ye think I can go about asking Miss Medenham if she seduced the Major?'

'A difficult conversation,' agreed the poet.

'I'm going to see Mr Patterson when we get back to town,' Miss Judith Fletcher said to her mother in a flat, hard voice.

'Why?' gasped Mrs Fletcher. Her cup danced on its saucer and the spoon tinkled.

'Because I want to buy a farm and breed horses. I'm not going to do this any more, Mother. I'm not going to marry Gerry. Why should I? He hasn't done me any harm. I managed to convince myself that I was in love with him but I'm not. I'm not going to be carted around like a slave and sold to the highest bidder. I'm not going to wear those blasted clothes and I'm never, never going to be the girl you want me to be.'

'Judy, you're mad!'

'No, Mother, I'm perfectly sane. I'm taking charge of myself. I've been a good girl for as long as I can remember. I've tried to be charming to boys I loathed and I've tried to be like you. But I'm not like you at all.'

'Get me my salts,' demanded Mrs Fletcher, falling back onto the sofa cushions. Judith took the slopping cup out of her feeble hand and applied salts ruthlessly, so that her mother choked and sat up.

'It doesn't matter what you say, Mother, and it doesn't matter if you go blue and faint. I'm moving out of your room and I'm seeing Mr Patterson as soon as we get back. You can stay in the house – I don't want it – and I'll make you some sort of living allowance, but I shan't be there to be humiliated any more.'

'You ... you unnatural daughter!' hissed Mrs Fletcher. Judith flinched but remained adamant. Phryne, listening unashamedly, had to suppress a cheer.

'You always wanted another husband, Mother, and someone might take you on if I'm not there.'

Miss Fletcher was clearly intent on stating everything which was on her mind, an unwise procedure at afternoon tea. Miss Mead, also eavesdropping, got up, wrapped her crochet in its silk scarf, and moved towards Mrs Fletcher, who was taking a deep breath in preparation for what would probably be a pyrotechnic display of hysterics.

'Come along,' murmured Miss Mead, putting a soft little hand on Mrs Fletcher's arm. 'I'll take you up to your room. This way, Mrs Fletcher. Come along. These family affairs are so trying,' she said, and somehow Mrs Fletcher found herself on her feet and out the door, cheated of her scene.

Phryne heard the shriek in the hall as Joan Fletcher realised this, and gave Miss Mead marks for social adroitness and courage.

Judith plumped herself down next to Phryne and announced, 'I told her.'

'I heard you. Now all you've got to do is hang on to your resolve and you'll be on your farm in a matter of weeks.'

'I owe it all to you.' Miss Fletcher seized Phryne's hand and shook it vigorously. Phryne retrieved her hand and counted the fingers. There seemed to be the usual number.

'My pleasure.' She swiftly interposed a plate of cream cakes between her and another embrace from a young woman with a grip like an ape.

'Thanks. Gosh, I can't imagine why I didn't do that years ago. I'm sorry about carrying on with your Mr Lin, Miss Fisher. I was only doing it to score off Gerry, and I didn't even want Gerry all that much. Golly, now I don't have to play at being a girlie any more. It's such a relief.' Her healthy complexion radiated robust gratitude.

'It would be. You're a good rider, Miss Fletcher. I saw you set out today, looking for the Major. Did you find any clue?'

'I caught his horse, trailing her reins, poor thing. Been ridden hard for a long way, poor creature could scarcely raise a trot. I had to tend her hoofs and walk her home. Mr Reynolds reckons that the Major must have gone into Buchan, though why I can't imagine. Gosh, Miss Fisher, I feel so fit. I think I'll take the hack out again and have a scout around.'

'Do that, but be careful. And don't go swimming.'

'No, I won't.' Her face flamed. 'I . . . was telling you the truth, you know. It didn't seem to matter if I lived or died.'

'But now you know that it does. Did you notice a stone tunnel in that little sandy bay on the river?'

'Yes, it's a drain or something. I didn't go near it. Gosh, is that the famous secret passage? Weren't you scared in the dark, Miss Fisher?'

'Not really. Now, you can get on with your life, Miss Fletcher. All you need to do is tell Gerry you won't marry him, and ask him to come and speak to me. Then talk to some stock suppliers about your horses.'

'I'll do that. And I'll send him to you.' Miss Fletcher bolted her cake. 'Doreen's moved my things into a little room, that's already done. You know, I've never slept alone in my whole life. First there was Nanny and then there was school and then there was Mother. It'll be nice, being alone. I think I'll like it.'

'I think you will.'

Miss Medenham in an afternoon-tea gown of flaming scarlet and Mrs Luttrell in her usual mousy wool came to the table for more tea.

'Miss Medenham, I have a question,' said Phryne. The bold eyes lifted. Miss Medenham was amused and very pleased with herself.

'If it is, "What did you do with the Major?" I can't answer. I didn't do anything with him.'

'You were close to him last night,' said Phryne delicately. 'Did he say anything about where he might have gone?'

'No, our conversation didn't touch on that. I suggested the Devil, but that might be farther than he could ride in one morning.'

Phryne turned to her companion. 'Mrs Luttrell?' The older woman cringed a little, out of habit, then straightened.

'He didn't come to me all night,' she said softly. 'I can't imagine where he is.'

But his absence is a great relief to you, as well it might be, Phryne thought. Something about the attitude of the two women, the way they were standing, indicated that an alliance had been forged. She occupied a few moments pleasurably, wondering what Miss Medenham had done to the Major. He seemed to have left the house under his own steam, so she hadn't actually crowned him with the fire irons. But that still left a broad scope for a woman of strong convictions.

Miss Medenham and Mrs Luttrell passed on through the crowd towards Doctor Franklin, who was talking to Tadeusz about hysteria.

Phryne accepted another cup of tea from Mrs Reynolds, who said worriedly, 'Two people missing and still those notes and things are unsolved. Have you got anywhere with them, Phryne?'

'Certainly. You will not receive any more notes. They were written on your own paper, you know.

It's the same as the paper in the office.'

'Will you tell me who was doing all these things?'

'Possibly. If you need to know. But the note-writer is not the murderer. And that will all be over. There is no threat to Tom, now. We just have to find Lina and the Major.'

'If you say so, Phryne.' The faded eyes looked into Phryne's.

'But you should prepare yourself for a shock,' said Phryne.

'Me?'

'Yes. I can only apologise in advance.'

Evelyn Reynolds searched Phryne's face for a clue as to what she meant. She seemed to have found something, for she looked sad. She opened her mouth to speak, then closed it again, nodding. Phryne held out a hand to the angelic Gerald, and Mrs Reynolds continued amongst the house party, dispensing tea.

'Well, Gerald?'

'Well, divine one?' He sat down on the floor at her feet and she caressed the curly hair as though he was a puppy. Jack Lucas, across the ornate parlour, scowled.

'So Judith won't marry you?'

'And that's a relief to us all. I suppose you wouldn't hear an honourable proposal? You should make an honest man out of me, you know.'

'You didn't need to sleep with me,' she said lightly, 'in order to enlist me. If you continue to do that every time you need a favour, then your lover is not going to be pleased.'

The whole body stiffened in shock. For a moment the brown eyes were blank with horror, then calculation took over.

'How could I have resisted you?' he asked, preposterously long eyelashes flicking down to the perfect cheek.

'Quite easily,' she said. 'It's all right, Gerald. I think I've fixed it. I have had a long talk with Tom Reynolds and although he won't give Jack any money ...' the soft mouth firmed into a thin line and Phryne lay one finger to his red lips, 'he'll give him something else of great value, which will be worth more than cash. I can't tell you any more until all this commotion with Lina and the Major is over, but I promise, on my honour, if Jack does not appreciate his legacy I will buy it from him and he will be able to live on the proceeds until he dies of old age.'

He scanned her face, made a decision, and said, 'I never meant you to be hurt, divine one.'

'I know you didn't. But you could have killed Tom and that wouldn't have been kind. I traced the ink and the paper on some of those notes, though not all.'

'I wanted the money for Jack and I thought ...'

'I know what you thought. Unfortunately your method was appropriated by someone else. By the way, have you been leaving urns all over the place?'

'No.'

'Good. I think someone's trying to help me, but so far I haven't worked out what they're trying to tell me. No more tricks, Gerry. I want your assurance, I want your word. It's all getting too dangerous.'

'I promise.' He wet his finger and traced a cross on his blazer. 'What ... what do you know about me, Miss Fisher?'

'I was in the boathouse,' she said gently.

All the living colour ebbed from Gerald's face, leaving him as pale as a porcelain faun. Phryne stroked his cheek. 'I was lying in a punt with Lin. I'm telling you, Gerry, your secret is safe with me and I will fix it. Now I need you to tell me exactly which of the tricks you played.'

'Three notes and the wire which brought Cuba down,' he muttered.

'Nothing more? You didn't saw through the axle? You sent no note to Lina? You were not out in the fog on the night she was attacked?'

'No. I was out, all right, but talking to ... the person you know of. Phryne, that time in the boathouse, that was the first time that we ...'

'I know. I heard everything you said.'

The boy kneeled up, his face close to Phryne's, and whispered, 'It wasn't just for a favour, Phryne. You were beautiful, you were lovely, I wanted you.'

'I know. I wanted you, too.'

'And you'll fix it for Jack if I'm a good child?'

'I will.'

Gerald smiled a breathtaking little-boy's smile. He took up Phryne's hand and kissed it. Rising with one smooth movement, he signalled to Jack

Lucas, and they left the room through the French window. Phryne heard them laughing outside.

'You seem to have improved their day,' commented Lin Chung, behind Phryne.

'I've saved their bacon,' she said. 'I've got a legacy for Jack and I've made Gerald promise that he won't play any more little jokes on Tom. That should clarify the situation.'

'It should?'

'Certainly. Lord, it's getting late. I'm going to have a nap before dinner. It's been an interesting day.' She smiled reminiscently.

'Mr Reynolds says that we are all going to Buchan Caves tomorrow. The dray is repaired,' said Lin Chung, stroking her wrist.

'Good. See you at dinner.'

'And after?' he asked, sliding one finger up her sleeve along the inside of her forearm where the skin was as thin as silk.

'And after,' said Phryne.

CHAPTER TWELVE

Now since these dead bones have already out-lasted
the living ones of Methuselah, and in a yard under
ground, and thin walls of clay, out worn all the
strong and specious buildings above it.

Urn Burial, Sir Thomas Browne, Chapter V.

DOT COLLECTED Phryne's early-morning tea and
met Li Pen's eyes as he loaded a cup onto his tray.
By mutual agreement they both came to the same
door, which Dot unlocked.

She walked across the room, drew the heavy
velvet curtains, and said, 'Morning, Miss Phryne.
It's a nice day.'

She pulled the curtains of the four-poster back
and stopped.

Like an engraving from a pillow book, thought
Li Pen. Like a painting from one of them old-time
artists, thought Dot.

Phryne, her black hair falling across Lin Chung's
chest, lay naked to the waist, turned so that one

small breast was bared to their gaze. One of her hands was curled open against his cheek, and his face had turned to her, so that Dot could see a stylised man; his nose and cheekbones, and the delicate black line of brow and eyelash and hair, as if drawn with a very fine brush. His other arm embraced Phryne even in sleep, long fingers splayed across her white back which was bruised from her fall.

'Hmm?' asked Phryne, swimming to the surface.

'Hmm,' agreed Lin Chung, waking all of a piece, languorous with pleasure. He noticed Dot's flabbergasted face and the appreciative countenance of Li Pen behind her. He was showing remarkable interest for a warrior-monk vowed to holy poverty, vegetarianism and chastity. But then Li Pen had always admired art.

'Silver Lady, we've got company,' said Lin, and Phryne woke. The picture dissolved. Dot handed her a robe and she sat up against Lin's chest to accept her cup.

'Good morning, Dot,' she said calmly. 'We're going to the caves. Are you coming, too?'

'Yes, Miss,' Dot replied. 'I've cleaned your clothes but they aren't dry. You'll have to wear the parrot jumper again, and the velvet trousers.'

'Fine.'

Li Pen said in Cantonese, 'She is as beautiful as the Manchu Princess of which you spoke, Master. More beautiful, because of her jade eyes.'

'Good, I'm glad you enjoyed the picture,' replied Lin. He repeated the remark to Phryne and she said, 'Thank you,' to Li Pen, who bowed. The whole transaction was so incredibly improper that Dot decided it had never happened.

Li dressed his master in a robe and Lin Chung took his leave. Phryne washed briefly in the wash-basin, pulled on her caving clothes, and went down to breakfast.

She was starving.

Breakfast was almost over when Mr Hinchcliff announced, 'Mr Jenkins,' and a strange figure was shoved into the breakfast room.

He was small, no more than five foot six, perhaps, and he appeared to be covered in hair. Phryne decided that he must have been cultivating his beard, which was of the general dimensions of a bathmat, since puberty and possibly before. The only person she had previously seen who was that furry was Jo Jo, the Dog-faced Boy. He was wearing moleskins and a blue shirt under a tweed jacket which had seen better centuries and was largely composed of patches. His feet occupied large hobnailed boots and his long wild hair was crowned with a shapeless felt bag which might, at a venture, have been called a hat. The modish colour of the season for swaggies, it appeared, was washed-out grey.

'Harry, my dear chap, sit down and have some breakfast,' called Tom Reynolds. So this was the famous Dingo Harry. Phryne hadn't recognised him without his trail of scalps. Tom Reynolds had obviously settled the quarrel about trespassing, probably in favour of Dingo Harry ignoring any boundary he wished to cross.

'Thanks, Tom. I haven't had a civilised breakfast for many a long year,' said Dingo Harry, giving Phryne her first surprise of the day. He spoke in a deep, pleasant, educated voice.

Dingo Harry was given free range amongst the edibles. He sat down next to Phryne, carrying his plate with some effort and setting it down carefully so that the bible-thick layer of ham would not fall off the edifice of toast and the scale model of Mont Blanc composed of scrambled egg.

Phryne watched him eat. This was usually instructive. She had seen wharfies and sailors eat as daintily as ladies, and ladies shovel food in as though they had spent a long day humping sacks up a gangplank. Dingo Harry secured his hair with a piece of string, then ate solidly but tidily through the whole menu. Then he wiped his mouth politely on a napkin, combed crumbs out of his beard and observed, 'You're Miss Fisher, the detective? You do nice work, Miss. I heard about the murder on the Ballarat train. Are you interested in caves?'

'Yes,' said Phryne, flattered at how far her notoriety had spread and perfectly prepared to be interested in caves if they proved interesting.

'Buchan Caves are a lump of Middle Devonian limestone that was once the bottom of the sea – it's very rich in marine fossils – sandwiched between the granite shelves on either side, so that they lie in a ring of mountains. All the interesting caves are limestone and there's hundreds of 'em here. That's why I originally came, to study the caves.' He gulped down his tea. 'Well, thanks for breakfast, Tom. Let's be going. Might I escort you, Miss Fisher?'

He offered his arm and Phryne took it. As they walked out of the house, she said quietly, 'I thought you would have seen me as a bloated member of the Capitalist classes,' and the man smiled, as far as one could see through the foliage.

'I've got a few friends and I hear things, even out here,' he said. 'Your maid talks to the kitchen staff and my old mate Terry hears and he tells me. You've got two friends who are red-raggers like me. You didn't instantly leap to the conclusion that I killed Lina, even though a wandering hermit tramp is a Godsend to anyone who wants a nice quick solution without revealing any family secrets.'

'Have you seen Lina or the Major?' she asked, and Dingo Harry shook his head. Either he hadn't, or he wasn't going to trust Phryne yet.

The dray had been repaired and even washed, and Terry Willis had prevailed on the carthorse to cooperate. Phryne was surprised to see that Paul Black was driving, large as life and twice as repulsive in an oilskin and hat. She let go of Mr Dingo's arm and grabbed her host's, asking, 'What happened about Black?'

'Can't throw him out for a joke, even a mistimed joke,' said Tom uncomfortably. 'I've docked his wages and he won't come near you or Lin again,

Phryne darling. There's no work in the countryside – I can't throw him out to starve or steal.'

'Can't you?' asked Phryne, and Dingo Harry chuckled.

'Always been soft, Tom,' he said.

'Now,' Dingo Harry told the assembled house party as the dray started with a jerk and they plodded along the road, 'these are the Buchan Caves. They weren't named after a place in Scotland, but after the Aboriginal word for dillybag, *bukken*. Because that's what they're like; a dillybag of limestone in the porphyry of the hills. Of course, there's an argument about the name. It might also be *bokkan*, which means plenty, or a form of *bakang*, which means dark. Anyway, they are made like this. Rain falls on a limestone shelf. There is nothing stronger than water.'

'Impeccable Taoism,' said Lin Chung.

Dingo Harry looked at him and nodded, continuing. 'Then the limestone weathers, see, because the rain picks up carbon dioxide from the air and forms a weak acid – carbonic acid. Limestone splits and dissolves and there are pits and holes and arches cut through it, until we have your basic cave. Then water drips through the roof. Each drop contains a minute amount of calcium carbonate, dissolved limestone, and it leaves a little ring of carbonate of lime on the stone. Everywhere the percolating waters form stalagmites and stalactites and dissolve the rock along fracture lines. After a while – twenty years, maybe – a stalactite begins to form. Water drips down that and the same thing happens when it hits the floor; a stalagmite, growing up. When they join in the middle they become a column. Sometimes, where the water lies in little hollows, the mineral calcite is precipitated, and that's a hexagonal crystal, making pyramids, or spread all over in little points of light. The basic colour of limestone is white. When there's an admixture of iron or other oxides, it's coloured. Now, we're going down. Have you all got torches?'

The party exhibited a variety of tow-wrapped torches and candles.

'Good. Don't stray away. It's black dark under the earth, darker than you've ever seen. Sound moves oddly in caves and it's very hard to find anyone who gets lost. Also, there are pits and shafts so deep they've never been plumbed, and they're full of icy water. We're going to Slocumbe's Cave. It was named after the man who found it. He was a grazier, a friend of Moon who was a prospector. Only a fifth of these caves have been excavated, and we're going to this one because it's nearest and deepest. We can't get to King's Cave, it's on the other side of the Snowy.' He flung out a hand. It was clearly impossible to get across the river. Between romantic chasms lined with trees taller than cathedrals, the river snarled and foamed, grey-blue water roaring through the abyss.

'*Where Alph, the sacred river ran, Through caverns measureless to man, Down to a sunless sea*', murmured Miss Mead, enthralled. Dingo Harry awarded her an approving look.

'That's where I found the bay mare,' observed Miss Fletcher, as the dray rocked and swayed on to a grassy siding next to the gravel road. A low opening with a barred gate in the side of a hill was visible. A small sign told them that this was SLOCUMBE'S CAVE NO TRESPASSING NO SHOOTING VISITORS PLEASE MIND YOUR HEADS.

'I hope Will Luttrell hasn't gone into the caves,' said Tom.

Dingo Harry remarked, 'If he has, only chance will find him.'

By this statement, Phryne learned that Mr Dingo was an atheist, as all the best red-raggers were, reserving their spiritual devotion for Marx and Engels. Paul Black drew the patient horse to a halt and let down the backboard, still grinning in a way which made Phryne itch to belt him with a picnic basket. Why on earth had Tom allowed this excrescence on the fair face of Australian labour to continue in his employ after his murderous assault on Phryne and Lin Chung?

She evaded Mr Black's greasy hand and leapt down from the dray without help. Dot followed, handing down Phryne's bag; a large leather pouch with a highly unfashionable shoulder strap. Miss Fisher had been trapped in the dark once and did not mean to encounter any confined spaces without adequate preparation.

Mr Black secured a nosebag to Dobbin's resigned countenance, put up the backboard, and sat down on the dray. He took out a clasp knife and a block of soft wood, and began to strip precise curls of bark off it, whistling 'Oh Susannah' through the remains of his teeth. Phryne turned her back on his slimy grin.

'Mind your heads,' said Dingo Harry as the party filed in through a passage some three feet wide and five feet high. Phryne, in the lead, had only to crouch a little, but the taller members of the group were bent almost double as they crept along the close-smelling tunnel and down an iron ladder bolted into the stone. Lin Chung, beside her, drew in a slow calming breath. Phryne remembered his fear of enclosed spaces.

'Wouldn't you rather wait outside?' she asked lightly. 'Nothing much to see down here and we won't be long.'

Lin, on whom the clay walls were closing in so that he could hardly breathe, would not be rescued. He said curtly, 'I'm sure that it will be most interesting,' and continued on. His face in the glare was as pale as limestone. Phryne gave him points for courage and, in charity, stopped watching him.

She wondered what strange concatenation of circumstances had brought Mr Slocumbe down this unpromising way. She was just deciding that he must have fallen in when she reached the floor and stepped away from the ladder. She switched on her electric torch and other lights sprang behind her as the rest of them came into the cavern.

It was vast. She could feel the elevation before she saw it. The ceiling was high, airy, and strangely figured. This might have been where the makers of Cave House had got their Gothic inspirations. Miss Fletcher said, 'I say!' and the poet gasped, '*Mère de Dieu!*'

It was as large as Westminster Abbey and decorated in rose, grey, white and salmon pink. Lengthy columns like melted wax candles as thick as Phryne's waist rose to unguessable heights. Across one corner was a sheet of pure white stone, almost as thin as cloth, which might have been expected to bear the Byzantine face of Christ. The moving lights across the floor combined in a sufficient glow to pick out formations like angels with spread wings, heraldic animals, and a wall of diamonds, shooting prismatic rays, which must be the mineral calcite.

It was like nothing that Phryne had ever seen; majestic and grotesque. The underground air struck chill, smelling of chalk and depths and cold water.

'Oh, wondrous,' murmured Lin Chung. 'Oh, water, mistress of earth, valley spirit, eternal feminine!'

'Taoism again?' Phryne leaned close to hear what he was whispering.

'From the *Tao Te Ching*. The old Master should have seen this. All made by water, the female, cold, moon principle.'

'Yin,' said Phryne. 'This is the womb of the earth.'

'Indeed.' He took her hand. 'Completely foreign to all male, hot, sun creatures.'

'Like you?'

'Like me. Yang can only admire and tremble.'

'Come along.' She led him into the centre of the huge space. 'We don't want to get lost in the earth-mother's insides.'

They followed the trail of lights across the floor to another tunnel, barely wide enough to fit Phryne and her bag. Lin's grasp on her hand tightened until it hurt. They came into a chamber of white stone, joined by a single slender column, and lined with basins of gems. A million facets threw back the different lights; cold electric-blue and white, warm-red, yellow and orange fire, dazzling the eyes. A trail had been trodden through gypsum roses, pink as any springtime, in the middle. Dingo Harry was in the lead, and Phryne could hear his voice, educated and rich, discussing the chemistry of limestone with Doctor Franklin as they walked through the rocky flowers up a gentle slope towards another dreamscape.

'They call this London Bridge,' said Dingo Harry.

They stopped in a body at a wide bridge, which looked like it had been thrown up by some convulsion of the earthmother as she turned in her sleep. It stretched, five feet wide and perhaps thirty feet long, over a chasm. 'Differential solution,' commented Dingo Harry. Someone, mindful of the nervous, had made a waist-high handrail out of hemp rope and pitons for the panicky to hang on to.

Phryne was not afraid of heights, and hung over the rope, listening to the millwheel churning of water in the depths below, and admiring the way that pink colouration gave way to bands of black and grey as the light receded down the walls of the cliff.

'Miss, Miss, be careful,' wailed Dot, who had shuffled across, holding on to the rope with both hands and resisting an unworthy urge to crawl.

The house party's variation in courage was interesting. Phryne noticed that Miss Mead and Miss Cray walked across without trouble, as did Mrs Reynolds and her husband and Li Pen, Miss Medenham and Mrs Luttrell. Mrs Fletcher baulked, caught her daughter's stern eyes, and managed the walk with only a subdued whimper. Dot didn't like it at all, whereas Lin Chung was utterly unafraid of heights, though he was not keen on depths. The poet had to be coaxed and the Doctor almost dragged. He was really afraid. Phryne saw a sheen of sweat on his bony face and his wide eyes caught the torchlight. Miss Fletcher almost led him over by the hand, talking to him gently as one would to a nervous horse. She seemed much more relaxed now that she did not have to strain at being a good girl. Phryne almost warmed to her as she and the Doctor went by.

As they passed through another junction, Phryne began to hear footsteps. They never coincided exactly with the noise the house party was making. Every time they all paused to survey some new marvel, the following feet tapped on a little longer than an echo would, then stopped.

She began to feel eyes on the back of her neck, and rubbed a palm over the prickling hair. Li Pen dropped unobtrusively back through the crowd until he stood beside Lin Chung. The slim valet said something to his master in Chinese and Lin replied quickly.

'Yes, I can feel it, too,' said Phryne, grasping at the meaning of the high, slurred dialect. She would never really get the hang of a toned language but she was beginning to pick up the sense of the speech.

Lin, surprised, said, 'You understood what he said?'

'Not really, but there's someone behind us. I can sense them.'

'You were certainly a warrior in a previous life,' said Lin. 'He says there is a wild animal in the cave. As this is Australia and I have assured him that there are no large predators here, he has decided that a human with the heart of a beast must be stalking us.'

'I almost wish you hadn't translated that. Li Pen, you remember the night we came here – is it the same hunter?'

Li Pen nodded. Phryne shook herself.

'We say nothing to the others,' she decided.

'But I go last,' insisted Li Pen. He fell in behind and followed as they walked into the new cave.

The sound of his cat footsteps behind her made Phryne feel much safer.

The new cave had teeth.

Instead of the massive, melted-looking columns

of the cathedral, this one was newer and the stalactites and stalagmites were almost sharp. They
dipped over Phryne's head like icicles, thin as
blades, striking up through the soft floor and
down from the roof like incisors, white as
bleached bone. It was a little unnerving and
Phryne felt Dot draw closer.

'In the mouth of the beast,' said Lin, and Phryne
snapped, 'Less mysticism and more light. If this
place was strung with electric lights it wouldn't be
so alarming. It's the contrast. White teeth and
black shadows.'

'You can't abolish all mystery with your modern
machines, Silver Lady. Some very old part remains;
some primitive Lin Chung who hid here when the
ice sheet moved down, and feared ghosts and bears
and shadows with fangs. He tried to fight his
terror with fire, also, and it did not entirely work.
If your electricity failed, the dark would return, as
it has been since the beginning of the world.'

'To banish fear with light has always been the
aim of humans,' agreed Tadeusz, breathing fast.
'Yet we cannot exile the shadows, for they lurk in
our own heart, our own mind.'

Phryne lifted her torch high, and the white teeth
gleamed with the dust of diamond. The stone on
her ring caught the light and blazed.

'Miss Fisher . . .' said Tadeusz, abandoning phil-
osophical speculation with a jolt. 'Wherever did
you get that ring?'

'I found it. Pretty, isn't it? Do you know it?'

'I do indeed. Though I haven't seen it for years –

diamonds are so seldom set in silver.'

'I think it might be Indian. What do you think?'

'No, it's South African. Miss Fisher, I don't think you should be wearing it, not in this gathering, it can only . . .'

Dingo Harry called them through into another cave. The poet lost his thread and said no more about the ring, although Phryne caught him glancing at it. She bit her lip in frustration.

The next cave was spacious and not too high, and the party sat down on convenient but damp stumps of stalagmites to drink tea and discuss what they had seen. Torches had been set in iron rings around the walls, and Phryne noticed that the smoke was blackening the pristine ceiling. Humans and caves did not go together. A few more years of human smirching and they would be sooty, smelly, grey and uninteresting. After which, presumably, humans would leave them alone, and the caves would repair themselves over a hundred years, patiently constructing more delicate alchemical marvels, to be ruined again by the next human who fell through the roof. Phryne was feeling most displeased with a species to which, she reminded herself, she belonged. She took an egg sandwich and a gulp of tea and strove to adjust her philosophy.

'What a remarkable place,' observed Miss Mead. 'A demonstration of the multifold gifts of the Almighty.' She trailed this unexceptionable tag at Miss Cray, who did not take her cue to launch into her usual speech on the Magnificence of God and the Necessity of Supporting His Work Amongst the Heathen with Immediate Generous Donations. Indeed she seemed altogether subdued, which would have been more interesting if Phryne had not felt as though something with talons was about to spring from the darkness onto her back.

'Yes, there are names for most of the formations,' Dingo Harry was saying in reply to a polite question from Miss Mead. 'This is called Picnic Cave, for obvious reasons. The first cave is called The Cathedral, and the formations are like the trappings of organised religion; The Pulpit, The Nave, The Font. Then there is London Bridge, Gem Cave, and Undersea Cave where the limestone is twisted into forms like fish and coral and weed. Surprisingly, the shapes are like those which would have been here when this was the bottom of the sea. See, here is a fossil, and another. Have a look at this wall.'

Phryne finished her sandwich and joined Tom Reynolds and the Doctor. The torchlight showed regular furrows, dips and indentations like shells and strange bubbles. She saw wavering shapes like weed and a fronded, primitive strand of kelp.

'Erinoids,' explained Dingo Harry, his scarred forefinger caressing the surface without actually touching. 'Don't touch them, please – the acid in your skin eats into the chalk. See, here is a shell, just like you'd find at the beach, and another one – and there is the important one.'

The wall appeared to be blank. Phryne unfocused her eyes and blinked. An armoured creature five feet long sprang into view. Dingo Harry's finger traced plates of shoulder and belly; the heavy, ridged, savage skull and the socket where a tin-plate eye must have gleamed. No room in that cranium for brain. Just reflexes, just the mindless hunting of any protein which moved. She saw it in a flash of insight, not frozen in grey stone but alive, slate-blue and monstrous, sliding through grey water like a pike or a shark, the lower jaw loose and shining with spiked teeth, the fins stroking lazily towards ... what? A floating baby in a leaf? Her own unprotected and terribly vulnerable limbs, unaware of the killer beneath the placid surface? A pounce, a swirl of blood which would bring all the lesser meat-eaters finning to the feast, a tearing gulp, and no more strange little heavy-headed mammal which might eventually have become a human.

Lin Chung, catching her mood, slid a warm hand into hers. Phryne called herself to order. It was unwise to indulge freely in imagination this far under the ground.

'It's an armoured fish – the first crocodile, you might say, though there's a lot of argument about that. Some say that sharks are the oldest, but they have no bones, they're cartilaginous, whereas this fellow was definitely bony, and well provided with teeth.' Dingo Harry's hand outlined the monstrous shape again. 'Life began in the ocean. Some experts suggest that the reason why no one's found the missing link is because humans went back to the sea when the earth dried up – the sea, in fact, is in our blood. The concentration of salt is exactly the same as sea water. It would also explain some of the human adaptations, the differences between us and the apes, our ancestors.'

Miss Cray did not even rise to this bait, which Phryne felt was unprecedented. Dingo Harry, who might have been expecting an interesting argument about the Creation, paused before he went on.

'Now, if we're all rested, we go through here on our way back.' He snuffed the wall torches and the shadows licked hungrily forward.

'In here,' he announced, leading the way into another cavern, 'is a cave known as The Crypt.'

'It certainly is,' agreed Phryne.

The cave was almost square, perhaps twenty feet high, and lined with blocks which strangely resembled tombs. Some past wag had inscribed names on some of them with a penknife which a vigilant mother should have confiscated before the lad became a vandal. 'Lillie Langtry' said one, and 'John Thomas' – someone had a rustic and earthy humour. Phryne walked the length of the cave with her torch, and the names sprang up in blue outlines like indelible pencil. 'Mary Ellis' got a mention, though if the writer had really loved her as he asserted, it seemed like a macabre joke. Limestone water dripped sadly, making strange echoes. A rising sun with the inscription, '1914 Steve Tom Albie'. Soldiers had come here and left this army badge in limestone, which was already blurring. 'Ronald Black'. 'The Boys Were Here'. 'Daisy, Bill and Johnno 1911'. Phryne wondered if they had ever come back again.

Some of the tables had occupants. Phryne saw draped figures lying on their last resting places, muffled in falling water which turned cloth into stone. Then she blinked and they were shapeless again. The floor crunched underfoot. She was destroying tiny precious crystals with her careless feet; with her human weight and warmth and breath, which had no place in this chill mausoleum.

'You see, this cave has all the accoutrements of a crypt,' Dingo Harry observed in some displeasure, clearly wishing that the earthmother had had better taste. 'Here is The Funerary Altar, and the stalagmites stand like candles upon it.'

This was true. The salmon-pink, grey and pale-yellow candles had obviously been burning for a few hours before they had frozen, flames alight, in stone. Miss Cray, who was possibly disordered in her wits, dipped into a genuflection as she passed them. Mrs Reynolds came to the old woman's side and took her arm. Phryne saw Dot cross herself almost without conscious volition. She herself was sobered and shaken by this underground place. She touched Lin and felt what he was feeling: the great weight and ancient bulk of the earth, pressing down over this unnatural hollow, groaning to be filled, bearing down, giving birth to boulders and rivers.

'Let's get out of here,' she said bracingly. 'I'm educated enough for one day.'

'I'm all right,' he said evenly.

'I know you are, but I'm not sure that I am.'

He smiled at her, the bronze face creasing into precise metallic folds in the cold light.

'The Altar, The Crucifix, The Censer,' continued Dingo Harry, leading the way out of the cave. The house party followed him close, eager to get back to the surface. 'And, of course, The Urn.'

'Oh, my God,' said Phryne, as they passed close to a massive cup-shaped rock formation. 'Lin, see if you can catch Tom Reynolds and bring him back without alerting the others. I know that smell of mortality.'

'Me, too,' muttered Dot, who had been to more funerals and lyings-in-state than was comfortable. 'Smells like a meat-safe on a hot day. Not putrid, yet, but getting that way.'

'That's what they were trying to tell me,' said Phryne slowly.

'Who?' asked Dot.

'Whoever it was who has been leaving urns about with such elaborate casualness. I'm afraid, Dot, that this is where the murderer took Lina's body. And I'm afraid . . .'

'So am I, Miss.'

Phryne was climbing up the side of The Urn. She almost lost her balance half way up when a scream echoed and re-echoed through the cave, and something ragged and insane with fear or fury erupted out of a tunnel into The Crypt.

CHAPTER THIRTEEN

Plaistered and whited sepulchres were anciently
affected in cadaverous and corrupted burials.

Urn Burial, Sir Thomas Browne, Chapter III.

Li pen crouched, Phryne dangled by both hands
from limestone as slippery as ice, and Tom
Reynolds caught the charging figure around the
shoulders and said, 'Will Luttrell! Where have you
been? We've been looking all over for you!'

'Dark,' shuddered the Major, struggling. 'Alone
in the dark. You, Tom, what're you doing here,
here of all places, why here?'

'We're on the way out,' soothed Reynolds. 'My
dear fellow, you're in a fearful state. How long
have you been wandering?'

'Don't touch me.' The Major threw off Tom
Reynolds' hand and swung a punch at him, which
missed. Then he sighted Phryne hanging from the
side of the rock formation called The Urn and
screamed, 'No! You can't go up there!'

'Yes, I can,' she said equably. 'Why, what do you think I'm going to find?'

'No!' He clawed at her ankles, and her fingers lost their grip. Phryne slid down the rock face swearing, as Li Pen came quietly up to the Major and applied a lock which pinned his arms to his sides. Mr Luttrell struggled, but did not seem able to move.

Dot stared at Lin Chung's man admiringly. No noise, no challenges, no man-to-man nose-to-nose confrontation or fuss. He just walked up to the recalcitrant Major and they were denatured before they knew what had happened. Li Pen, for his part, was disappointed that so far in his sojourn in Australia, he had never met anyone who knew anything about real fighting. His master had told him that a warrior needs challenges or he grows complacent.

The rest of the party had come back into The Crypt, attracted by the noise. They crowded through the doorway and stopped as they saw Phryne ascending The Urn and Li Pen holding the fuming soldier with negligent ease.

'What on earth . . .' began Mrs Reynolds, and the poet swore in some obscure tongue. Li Pen brought his prisoner forward.

'Not there!' yelled the Major. 'Don't let her go up there!'

The smooth stone was very hard to climb. Phryne could get to the bulge which marked the middle of formation but no further. Her fingers slipped on the smooth sides and she could not find a foothold. She was, however, sure of what she would find; the charnel-house smell was stronger the higher she climbed. Meat of some sort was spoiling in The Urn.

As she clung to the protrusions in the stone, considering which might bear her weight for a short time, she was almost shaken down by a dreadful noise; a crack, whine and boom. The company were driven together like sheep threatened by a dingo.

Someone had fired a gun. A large-bore hand gun, probably a .45, reflected Phryne, edging around out of the immediate line of fire. A figure carrying a torch in one hand and a gun in the other came into sight behind The Altar. A breeze blew in and gusted the flame. Phryne realised that there must be another tunnel.

It was Paul Black, all grease and smile, and he stood for a moment surveying the house party with arrogant ease.

'Stand still,' he said.

The appearance of the gunman had started movement in the crowd. Lin Chung had taken one quiet pace into deep shadow. Miss Mead had seen him go and immediately turned her back, taking Miss Medenham's arm and compelling her to move with her. Phryne clung to the obverse of The Urn, out of sight. Mrs Fletcher began to scream, a high, thin wail, until she was shocked into silence by Miss Fletcher striking her across the face. She subsided into frightened sobbing. Tom Reynolds shoved to the front with Evelyn at his shoulder, presenting, Phryne thought, a magnificent target. Dingo Harry stood beside him, beard bristling with fury. Mrs Luttrell had not rushed to her husband, who had been silently released by Li Pen, but sidled close to Miss Medenham. Gerald and Jack Lucas edged together and Phryne saw their shoulders touch, though they did not look at each other. Li Pen had, like his master, faded as far as possible into the dark at the edge of the gathering. Doctor Franklin gaped, wiping a hand over his forehead as though he was running a fever, while the poet, who had presumably seen both guns and revolutionary outrages before, held both hands away from his body and tried not to catch the mechanic's eye. Dot stiffened with offence and stared at Paul Black, elaborately not glancing in Phryne's direction.

'You're all my prisoners,' gloated Mr Black.

'What's the meaning of this? How dare you?' yelled Tom Reynolds. 'Put that gun down!'

He dived forward and Paul Black lowered the sights and fired.

There was the dreadful noise again, a stench of cordite, and Tom Reynolds fell, shoved backward by the force of the bullet. His wife leapt to his side, cradling him in her arms. The Doctor immediately dropped to his knees to examine the injury. He pulled away the shirt and revealed a bloody wound in the upper-chest and shoulder. Tom groaned.

'That will happen again if anyone tries to attack me,' announced Mr Black.

'Is he dead?' whispered Miss Medenham.

'No, but it's a nasty wound. One of you ladies, give me your petticoat,' snapped the Doctor. 'Mrs Reynolds, hold him up a bit so that he doesn't choke. Someone give me a knife. We need to get that coat off him.'

'You pay attention to me!' yelled the gunman, brandishing the weapon.

'You've got us,' snapped the Doctor. 'But unless you mean to shoot us all, I will tend to my patient.'

Phryne cheered silently behind her rock. Miss Fletcher said, 'Bounder!' and Jack Lucas said, 'Good show, Doctor.'

'You, Lucas, come here,' sneered Black, and Lucas gave Gerald a long glance. Their hands met, unseen by the house party. Jack straightened, walked to the foot of The Altar and said, 'Yes? What do you want, my man?' in his best born-to-rule drawl, obviously calculated to provoke working-class fury. Phryne held her breath, but Paul Black did not react except to laugh.

'I want this party secured. There are ropes in Dingo Harry's kit – he always has ropes. You and Gerald can begin tying everyone up. Hands behind the back and ankles together. I'll kill anyone who struggles.'

'No,' said Jack Lucas, after deep thought. He looked into the pistol barrel as it came up, aimed at his head. 'You want to use me as your instrument to control us all,' he said calmly. 'I can't see that doing your bidding would keep me alive, much less the people I love. If you're going to shoot me, you can shoot me now. I can't stop you.'

Paul Black raised the gun and Phryne saw his finger tighten on the trigger.

'Jack, no!' wailed Gerald, running to his side. 'I'll do it, I'll do it,' he gabbled, dragging a coil of thin rope out of Dingo Harry's bag. 'Just don't hurt us.'

'Oh, Gerry,' mourned Jack.

'You've got to live,' said Gerald, looping a line around his friend's wrists and tying it tight. 'We've got to live.'

'This isn't the way,' said Jack. Paul Black leaned down and struck him across the face with the gun. Jack staggered and fell to his knees. Gerald whimpered over him, smearing blood over the injured cheek and his own.

'You, get up,' ordered Mr Black. 'Tie up the others or watch your friend die.'

Gerald took up the line and began to truss the rest of the company into bundles. When he came to Miss Mead, he whispered, 'Don't look at me like that, I can't bear it.'

'How was I looking at you?' she asked.

'Like I'd let you down. Don't, please. I want us to live.'

'So do I, young man,' said Miss Mead, allowing him to secure her hands and feet. 'So do we all.'

Miss Cray allowed herself to be tied. Miss Medenham and Mrs Luttrell did not struggle, though Miss Medenham whispered, 'You wait until we get out of this, my lad, I'll thrash you with my own hands.' The poet submitted with a few Finno-Ugric curses, and the Major fought. He was half mad with isolation and fear and he was very strong. Gerald could not hold him and no one else came to his assistance. Major Luttrell struck Gerald with an open hand and sent him flying against the wall.

Paul Black came down from his eminence. This was the predator, the human with the heart of a beast that Li Pen the hunter had sensed. Phryne wondered how she had ever found Mr Black negligible. He was glowing with dark pleasure, as though their submission and his power fed some black strength inside him. Phryne for the first time began to feel that they were all in danger of immediate death, and to wonder if she could make it to the top of The Urn without too much noise. She had her little gun in her bag, but a shoot-out in the cave would be far too dangerous. The candles were burning down, there were no fixed torches, and a stray bullet might find any lodgement.

The Major was shouting fragments of sentences and struggling wildly. Paul Black stood above him, growling, 'You stupid old bastard,' and struck him across the head with the gun butt. The Major fell silent. Gerald tied him up with hands that shook so much that he could hardly form a knot.

'Where's Miss Fisher and the Chink?' demanded Paul Black, who seemed to be counting.

'They're still in The Cathedral. They had ... other concerns,' said the poet quickly, and smiled a lecherous smile. 'You know what they say about Chinese. That's why there are so many of them.'

Mr Black grinned. Phryne gave Tadeusz a gold star for lightning acuity, doubtless polished during the riots in Paris. A sinful explanation was always convincing.

By scoring holds in the soft stone with her knife, she had managed to clamber to the top of The Urn. As she had expected, a corpse lay in the hollow centre of the stone, soaking in mineral-laden water, cradled in gemstones. A thin limestone crust had formed over Lina's face, greying her skin and hair and the sculptural folds of her nightdress. In twenty years, Phryne thought, the body would be entirely enclosed in stone, and they would call the formation 'Sleeping Beauty', perhaps, or '*L'Inconnue*', the beautiful suicide pulled out of the Seine whose placid plaster countenance graced a thousand Parisian mantelpieces.

Death, cold, or the chalky droppings had smoothed away the angry swollen bruises of Lina's body, so that the countenance was almost peaceful. The lipped hollow looked strong, and Phryne clambered over the top and knelt next to Lina, hoping that they were both still out of sight.

'What do you want with us?' growled Dingo Harry.

'You don't know who I am,' said Black, 'and you won't know. I'm going to claim my money, so that means you all have to die.'

'If you had just wanted us dead, you wouldn't have gone to all this trouble,' said Miss

Medenham. He walked through the huddled shapes and straddled her like Appollyon. She glared into the dark eyes defiantly. 'There must be more to it.'

'Oh, there is,' he said softly. A greasy hand with broken nails reached down and tore her dress, quite deliberately, then ripped the undergarment, leaving her breasts bare. Tom Reynolds tried to bellow and fell back on to his wife's shoulder. Mrs Luttrell, who was tied next to Miss Medenham, said, 'Cynthia . . .'

'Hush, Letty. Close your eyes, now,' said Miss Medenham quickly. 'I'll be all right. Don't look.'

'Paul, don't do this,' urged Tom Reynolds.

'Why not?' asked Mr Black.

There was no answer to that. Miss Medenham twisted, thrusting out her bosom, her eyes locked on the dirty face. She almost seemed to be enticing him. She did not wince as the mouth fixed on hers and his weight crushed agonisingly down onto her body and her hands bound behind her back.

This could not be allowed to continue. Phryne called, 'I wouldn't do that,' and Paul Black straightened and snarled.

'Where are you?'

'I'm everywhere,' said Phryne, speaking at the ceiling so that her voice echoed.

'Who are you?'

'I'm Lina,' she said.

Paul Black stood up, leaving Miss Medenham to drag in a deep breath of relief and rub her soiled face on Mrs Luttrell's shoulder.

'Tart,' observed Miss Cray, coming to life. 'Slut. Whore.'

Paul Black kicked her into silence and addressed the air.

'You never came, Lina,' he accused.

'I was prevented,' said the sad, high voice.

He stalked towards The Altar, gun in hand, quivering with strain.

'What stopped you?'

'A man,' said Phryne, pitching her voice as high as she could to mimic the dead woman's tone. 'Harry rescued me.'

'Harry did?'

'I fired my shotgun at a struggling couple, that real foggy night,' remembered the old man. 'The girl was screaming, "Let me go!" and I wanted her attacker to do just that. I only fired one shot. But by the time I got up to them, they were gone.'

'Lina? Where are you, Lina? Come out!' bellowed Paul Black.

'Shan't,' said Phryne, petulantly. 'You never came. I waited for you and you never came.'

Paul yelled, 'Come out!' and fired a shot into all four walls, one after another, then into the roof, laughing as the echoes cracked and died. The house party, who could not cover their ears, rolled in pain, which made their captor laugh again.

He's fired six shots and he should only have six, thought Phryne. However, I can't identify the make of pistol from here. And he's probably got a pocketful of ammunition. She had seen the reason now for Miss Medenham's display of pulchritude. Lin Chung was lurking in the shadows, though he might be almost frozen with claustrophobia by now. Miss Medenham had clearly seen him and was trying to lure the gunman close enough for a pounce, but to Phryne's eyes Lin was too far away. The floor of the cave was coated with tiny crystals which crunched like sand underfoot. Lin Chung would have been heard and shot in mid-spring. She could not see Li Pen at all. Tom Reynolds moaned and Phryne smelt blood even stronger than powder. Something would have to be done soon before poor Tom bled to death.

'I'm here,' she cooed, getting her shoulder under the corpse. The body was heavy and floppy and Phryne hoped that she herself would neither faint nor vomit. She allowed the face to show over the high lip of The Urn and Paul Black ran towards the formation.

'Lina, we'll go away from here, we'll never come back. I promise I'll never leave you again. Come down,' he said, and Phryne exerted all her strength and shoved the body down out of The Urn into Paul Black's extended arms.

A blur from one side of the cave, a rush from the other, and the gunman, sinking under the weight of a dead woman, was seized and pinioned before he knew what had happened.

Li Pen held one arm, Lin Chung the other. Gerald came forward with a length of rope and secured Paul Black. He did not appear to notice. The satanic fit had passed. He crumpled to the cave floor, staring at the ruin of Lina's face, wailed with unbearable grief and retched with horror.

'Gerald, undo everyone immediately,' ordered Phryne, climbing carefully down. 'And before we lynch Gerald, let us remember that we have all survived.'

'He tied us as loosely as he dared,' commented the poet, freeing his own hands. 'He did the best he could. And we have survived.'

'Praise God,' said Miss Mead, and Miss Cray echoed her.

'Well done, Miss Medenham. You almost had him trapped, but I think Lin Chung was too distant,' said Phryne loudly, helping the woman up.

'God, and I almost had him, too,' replied Miss Medenham, shuddering. 'He would have gone on with it – he was mad with power. Ugh, I can still feel his filthy hands on me. Is there any tea left in the basket? I want to wash my mouth out. Oh, disgusting. It'll be days before I can bear to be kissed again.' She caught the poet's congratulatory gaze and grinned. 'Well, hours.'

'How are you, Tom?' asked Phryne, noticing that the red stain was growing on Mrs Luttrell's petticoat.

'All right,' grunted her host.

'The bleeding's slowing,' said Doctor Franklin. 'It's not serious.'

'See? Only a flesh wound, like in the movies,' Tom said to his desperately worried wife.

'It's time to explain,' said Phryne. 'Break out the brandy we brought along for medicinal purposes and hang on to that madman. If I don't sort this out I don't feel I can bear to see grass and sky again. Give me his gun,' she requested.

The poet retrieved it and she broke it open. 'Eight shots,' she said faintly.

Jack Lucas and Gerald were talking quietly, and in the sudden silence, as Phryne contemplated how close they had come to eternity, she heard Jack say sadly, 'It's just how you are, Gerry. You can't help it. I can either take you or leave you. You'll never change.'

'And what do you choose?' asked Gerald, almost under his breath.

'I choose to take you, of course,' said Jack. He brought up his warm hand and stroked the bruised cheek. Gerald, relieved, burst into tears.

'Everyone find a seat, light the rest of the torches, pass the bottle around. Dot, fetch my bag, a handkerchief and the eau de Cologne, if you please. Are you all right, old thing?'

'Yes, Miss,' said Dot. 'I knew we'd be all right. You were up on that Urn and I could see Mr Li in the shadows. Here you are, Miss.'

Phryne saturated the handkerchief in the spirit and passed the bottle to Miss Medenham, who took a swig, spat, and scrubbed at her lips. Mrs Fletcher found the relief of being rescued too great, and fainted. Her daughter pillowed her mother's head on a convenient rock and took her turn at the brandy bottle. Lin Chung, holding on to one of Black's arms, said to his bodyguard in Cantonese, 'It might have worked.'

'Never. You were too far away,' said Li Pen. 'You would have been shot and then what would I tell your father?'

'What you should be worrying about is what you would have told Grandmother.'

Both of them fell silent, shuddering.

Phryne sat herself on a conveniently central tomb and began.

'I came to this house to have a nice little holiday and to solve a small mystery,' she said. 'My host was getting blackmailing notes from someone who said they had been cheated out of an inheritance. Everyone thought it must be Jack Lucas, and some of the notes were sent on his behalf, though not by him or with his knowledge. The others, however, were not. All of them were written in black ink on typing paper taken from the office at Cave House. I was almost killed by a trip-wire and there has been a fair bit of damage and petty mischief around the place. I worked out who was doing some of it, though not all, and that was again a matter which led to no bad effects and need not be considered, especially since I have effected a settlement of the Lucas issue which is acceptable to both parties.'

Gerald drew a deep, quiet breath and leaned on Jack's shoulder.

'There were other mysteries. Someone kept leaving urns in my room, and my friend's, clearly trying to tell us something. What had happened to Lina in the fog, why was she out there, why wouldn't she say who attacked her, and where was

— 232 —

her body? Because I had an advantage over the rest of you, I had seen her corpse, I knew that she was dead, while to the household at large she was just missing, and maids can be missing for a variety of reasons.' Jack Lucas passed Phryne the brandy and she took a gulp.

'Someone clearly knew when Lina was expected to recover and to be able to tell us what had happened. The people who knew this were me, the Doctor, Tom, the Major, and Mr Black, who was passing at the time with a lot of leads on the way to mend a flex.'

All eyes turned to the fallen gunman, who did not react. Phryne surveyed the faces. The house party had made up their minds.

'I thought of the Doctor,' she went on. 'He might have reasons to kill Lina, especially if he had assaulted her. There were rumours that he had been too friendly with some of his more sensitive and wealthy female patients.'

Doctor Franklin stiffened and said, 'That is an outrageous suggestion!'

'Isn't it? And fairly unlikely, too. However, you were playing chess with Mr Lodz at the right time. Tom and the Major were supposed to be fishing. That seemed to rule out both of them. But, it turned out, my host had felt his old bones aching and had come back early to play billiards with Gerald and Jack. Mrs Croft told Dot that the Major caught no fish – the trout at dinner were captured by the stableboy and Albert, who proudly produced them in an attempt to buy off punishment for skiving when they should have been working. So it might have been the Major after all. He certainly seemed the best candidate for a midnight rapist. He had *droit de seigneur* in India over the house staff, flirted with every available female and yet treated his wife like a slave. Like most men bent on conquest, he profoundly disliked women.

'Anyway, I saw the body, closed the door, and came to get Mrs Reynolds. In the space of time it took to track her down in the kitchen garden, Doreen cleaned the room, abolishing a lot of valuable clues. Someone in muddy boots who knew the house walked in, took the body, walked out and into the secret passage, laying the body in a marble sarcophagus in the cellar. I favoured the Major, and such was the case. Wasn't it, Major? You knew that she would come if you sent a note signed R, because the girl was in love with Ronald, the disgraced son of the house, and she'd never believed that he was dead. You sent the note, intercepted her in the fog, and assaulted her. Poor Lina. She came expecting to see the man she loved, and she got you instead. She screamed and Dingo Harry, springing to the defence of an oppressed daughter of the labouring classes, fired that shotgun blast. I heard it and I rescued the girl. She wouldn't have had a chance otherwise, would she, alone in the fog with a murderer?'

'He killed her?' demanded Paul Black hoarsely, never taking his gaze from the dead girl's face.

'Oh, yes, he killed her,' said Phryne flatly.

'She was mine. She flaunted herself at me, begged me to take her, then she screamed, like all women, bitches, all bitches.' The Major stopped speaking. Li Pen tightened his grip on his neck.

'Lina was in love with Ronald?' asked Mrs Reynolds, shocked.

'Oh, yes. She loved him before he went away. He gave her this ring, told her he'd love her forever, then went off to wherever it was he went. Then he came back, of course, and began writing letters, demanding his inheritance.'

'He came back? Where is he?' demanded Mrs Reynolds.

'He's here,' said Phryne. She walked over to Paul Black and pulled his head round by the hair. She applied the cologne-soaked handkerchief to his face, scrubbing vigorously. He bit at her hands until Lin Chung laid one fingertip very gently to his eyelid, after which he froze. Phryne cleaned busily, using up two handkerchieves and the last of the scent.

Then she wiped at the fringe which was flopping over his forehead, and black grease or dye came away. The actual colour of the hair was brown.

'There. Do you know him?' asked Phryne, allowing Lin and Li to drag Paul Black to his feet.

Mrs Reynolds made a dreadful, heartbroken noise and her husband clutched her.

'Oh, Ronald,' she whispered. 'Oh, my son.'

'He has been in prison, which puts lines on the face,' observed Phryne. 'And someone tried to take out his eye with, at a venture, a bottle. The scar distorts his mouth. No one would know him from his photographs when he was a young ne'er-do-well and the spoiled son of a great house. An excellent disguise, which he added to with judicious applications of grease. Fooled almost everyone. Not Lina, of course, because she knew him the moment he arrived. Didn't you think it odd, Tom dear, that such a well-skilled mechanic would want to come all the way out here and work for you? Of course you did. You wouldn't take the attack on Lina seriously because you thought Ronald had done it. You knew, my dear, didn't you?'

'Not at first,' protested Tom. 'I didn't know he was Black. I just knew he was here, somewhere.'

Mrs Reynolds said, 'Tom?'

'Yes, yes, m'dear. I was trying to think of a way to tell you, I really was. But I knew it would grieve you so terribly. I was waiting for him to approach me, stop sending those notes, so I could offer him some money to go away. He never did. I didn't know about Lina. Of course, he wanted to take her with him.'

'But then she was killed. I thought Ronald found the body and brought it here, but now I don't know.'

'I brought her,' snarled the Major. 'I made . . . someone . . . help me.'

'Oh? Why didn't you just fling the body in the river?'

'Might have fetched up. That pool up there is a petrifying well, so the body would stay there, a monument. Poor fools would find her after fifty years and know that she was mine, my mark still on her, and they'd make up stories about the poor girl lost in the dark, who lay down in the cool water and died. But I'd know how she came to be there. I put her there. My creature. Entirely mine,' announced the Major. His wife stared at him in utter loathing. Phryne went on.

'You see, Tom dear, you had a houseful of secrets and that played into the disgusting Major's hands. He knew everything about everyone, probably from the observant Miss Cray, whose confidence could be easily purchased with a hefty donation to her favourite cause. Almost everyone had something to lose. Reputation or honour or some secret that they could not bear to have haled out into the light. Those whom his overwhelming character could not daunt could be blackmailed into silence. Do you realise that he walked through the whole house, down those stairs and out through the back door, without anyone daring to say that they had seen him? God knows what he had on Miss Medenham – perhaps she might tell us later. She saw him pass the library door and said nothing. Jack Lucas and Gerald Randall had their own reasons for silence. Tadeusz wasn't there, but he has his weak spot also. Miss Cray – you know, don't you? Miss Mead?'

'Oh, yes, dear.' Miss Mead, unruffled by adventure, looked as though she regretted not bringing her crochet.

'I thought you did, from that remark about the

Acts of the Apostles. Ananias and Sapphira failed to turn all their worldly goods over to the Lord and he struck them down – a fable that soured me on the entire New Testament. Miss Cray's a thief, isn't she? All that money went to the Make Miss Cray a Rich Lady Fund, didn't it?'

'Oh, yes, Miss Fisher,' said Miss Mead collectedly. 'I am concerned in a lot of little charities, and no one knew anything about Miss Cray, not even the more ... er ... extreme sects.'

'No!' shrieked Miss Cray. 'The heathen ... the heathen ...'

'Yes, yes, dear, of course,' murmured Miss Mead. 'Just sit down on this nice stone and have some tea.'

'Miss Fletcher was playing tennis with Lin at the time, but Mrs Fletcher failed to notice a fifteen-stone military gentleman carrying a rolled blanket over one shoulder. This may have something to do with Miss Fletcher's trust fund, and the uses to which some of it has been put. It was not until I had lit a fire under Miss Fletcher that her mother realised that her comfortable existence was threatened by a palace revolution. Silk hangings for your boudoir, I believe you said, and a tour of Europe every year? The Major had encountered you on several trips, and someone had told him that Miss Fletcher's money was supposed to be spent on Miss Fletcher. Still, I suppose it's lucky you didn't put it all into Megatherium. But you aren't strong enough to carry Lina's body anywhere, so I had to discount you, much as I think you have the right kind of mind to be a murderer.'

Mrs Fletcher, having recovered enough to hear this dispassionate speech, fainted again and her daughter replaced her head on the rock. Phryne continued.

'Doctor Franklin – yes, you fit. The Major clearly has a lot of these little extra-marital adventures, and he would need the services of a good abortionist. That is the *raison d'être* of your chain of nursing homes, isn't it, Doctor? There is nothing wrong with your trade.' Phryne held up a hand to still a protest. 'You perform a valuable public service. There was that scandal a few years ago, though, wasn't there, when that girl died? And I believe that your fees are very high. It must cost you a fortune to pay off the cops, though you would have friends in high places. No wonder you have neurasthenia. Illegal operations are so nerve-wracking. So you helped the revolting Major to carry his hunting trophy here, did you?'

The Doctor, almost sinking with shame, nodded.

'And there are other secrets. Only Lin, Miss Mead and I appear to be without them. The poet is not who he seems, eh, Tadeusz? You should polish your cigarette case and disguise your seat on a horse. But that can wait. You all covered up for the Major, and we can perfectly understand it. Now is the time for us all to forgive ourselves and leave this dark place. I don't know how long it'll be until we can get a policeman out from Bairnsdale, but we've got a commodious cellar for you gentlemen, and I'm sure that you have a lot to talk about to while away the long darkness.'

Lin and Li stood Ronald up. He hoisted the dead body of Lina into his arms. His mother came to him, and he snarled at her, so that she jumped back as if she had been confronted with a wild dog.

'I came back, Mother,' he said through bared teeth. 'Aren't you glad to see your little boy?'

'Ronald, why didn't you tell me?' she pleaded, stroking the dirty hand.

'You never knew me, you never even looked at me, Mother,' he said. 'I just came back to get my rights, and to find Lina again. She loved me. She was a skivvy, Mother, a servant, and she knew me right away, the moment Paul Black walked through the door. I never cared what happened to him.' He jerked his head at Tom, walking shakily but under his own steam. 'But I thought you'd know.'

'What did you mean to do?' asked Phryne, as they passed into another cavern, a four-foot broad flat ledge over a deep pit.

'I meant to go back to America. I meant to take Lina with me. But I can't do that now. It's all ruined. That bastard, that bloody bastard killed her.' His lip quivered. 'But if I can't take my girl with me one way,' he said, 'I can do it another.'

He threw the corpse away, into the air, and then seized the Major in an unbreakable grip. Phryne hissed, 'No, Lin, come back,' as the Chinese grabbed at the struggling pair.

Phryne heard Lina's cadaver strike the bottom of the pit; a dull thud. Paul Black had the Major by the neck and the Major grappled Black by the waist. They panted and stamped, purple face to purple face, while Phryne, Lin and Li Pen flattened themselves back against the wall. Mrs Reynolds screamed, 'My son!', Dot called, 'Look out!' and, almost in slow motion, they fell.

Phryne saw the murderers, clasped as close as lovers, topple off the lip of the limestone bridge and fall, inseparable, into the abyss.

CHAPTER FOURTEEN

And therefore restless disquiet for the diurnity of our
memories unto present considerations seems a vanity
almost out of date, and superannuated piece of folly.

Epistle Dedicatory, *Urn Burial*, Sir Thomas Browne.

SUNLIGHT HAD never looked so bright nor crushed
grass smelt so sweet. The house party dragged
themselves up the iron ladder and out into the light.
Phryne threw herself down almost at the feet of the
horse, who snuffled politely at her hair and
courteously refrained from standing on this strange
human who was rolling down a slight slope to come
to rest on her back, staring up at the sky.

Dot dumped the picnic basket into the cart and
observed, 'Miss Phryne?'

'Here. This grass smells lovely.'

'Yes, Miss.' Dot considered that all grass smelt the
same. Sort of grass-scented. Her eccentric employer
rubbed her filthy face on the pasture, rolled over,

and sat up, picking burrs out of her hair.

'Quite. I suppose we'd better be going. Have we got everyone?'

'I think so, Miss. Is Mr . . . er . . .' it did not seem quite polite to call him Dingo Harry, but Dot didn't know his other name. 'Is Mr Dingo coming with us?'

'He certainly is,' said Miss Medenham, who had a firm grip on the retiring geologist's patched jacket. 'We owe him a bath and a good dinner at least.'

Lin and the Doctor helped Tom Reynolds into the dray.

'I'll drive,' offered Tadeusz. Phryne packed herself in beside Lin and leaned on his shoulder. He put an arm around her.

'That was a dreadful ending to the story,' she said quietly.

'But a fitting one. Divine Justice would dictate it.'

'As Proverbs says, "He that diggeth a pit shall fall therein",' observed Miss Mead. 'What would have happened if the Major had survived, or Paul Black – pardon, Ronald – to tell their story? Ruin and scandal and the wreck of innocent lives. Far better that they are dead and with God, who will know how to deal with them. That is, after all,' Miss Mead said gravely, 'what God is *for*.'

'Indeed,' said Dingo Harry, devoutly.

The return of the house party was marked by a drain on the hot water supplies and a clumping together of people for mutual comfort, expostulation, or absolution. Miss Cray scuttled to

Miss Mead's room to explain what had happened to the church funds. Gerald and Jack, in dressing-gowns, locked themselves into a second-floor bathroom and were incommunicado for more than an hour. Miss Fletcher had a quick wash, scaled the stairs, and hit a tennis ball with great verve against the Cave House dome. Mrs Fletcher was laid down on her bed by her expostulating maid who applied smelling salts and brandy. The poet, Miss Medenham, the Doctor and Mrs Luttrell took over the parlour, smoking cigarettes and sitting close by each other on the huge couch, playing the gramophone and drinking cocktails. Tom Reynolds was escorted to his room, pronounced in need of rest, and put firmly to bed. His wife, in defiance of all custom, shut the door at two in the afternoon and lay down on his unwounded side, crying for her lost son, now definitely dead and gone.

Dingo Harry carried the news of the terrible events at the caves to the kitchen, where he was supplied with endless tea and his favourite cakes as he held the staff agog. Mrs Croft made scones and the kettle boiled, and no one could understand why Doreen sat mute in a corner, would not even taste a morsel, and looked likely to weep.

Phryne and Lin Chung climbed the monumental stair, too tired even to react to the decor. They washed briefly and lay down naked together in the big bed, flank to warm flank, talking quietly.

'At least you'll be here,' said Phryne to Lin.

'Riddles,' he sighed into her hair. 'When will I be here?'

'When the nightmares come. I'll see it all again. The grip of the hands, the wrestling bodies, and that slow, inevitable fall.'

'I'll see that, too. It is a matter of endurance. Eventually, the memories fade, Silver Lady.'

'I know they will. It's just that the process is not comfortable.'

'You comfort me,' he said sleepily.

'You comfort me,' she replied.

Dot took Li Pen to the kitchen and supplied him with hot sweet tea and scones with strawberry jam. She had decided that he needed feeding. And she wanted to ask him if he would teach her how to put on that paralysing armlock. It was a thing any girl in 1928 might need to know.

Phryne sensed the sweetish smell of rotting flesh again and felt the flaccid corpse in her arms, the head lolling against her breast. She jerked herself out of a drowse and stroked the real head reposing on her shoulder, touched dry warm skin with the pulse of life in the throat. His mouth opened as she touched it, kissing her fingers.

'Shadows, Silver Lady,' said Lin Chung, waking up and embracing her.

The party in the parlour had become raucous and drunken. Miss Medenham was dancing a tango with the Doctor when Phryne came in, dressed for dinner in her jade gown. She reflected that if Miss Medenham got any closer to Doctor Franklin they would be wearing the same dress, and that brilliant scarlet might be a little trying for Doctor Franklin's complexion. Hinchcliff handed her a cocktail.

'My special recipe!' exclaimed Tadeusz, grinning, from his place next to Mrs Luttrell on the sofa.

Phryne sipped cautiously. The cocktail was, perhaps, Slavic. It seemed to be compounded of absinthe, noyau and cherry brandy, a combination she had not heard of before. It was remarkable. She gulped it down while she was still undecided about the taste and sat down rather quickly under the impact.

The newly made widow was not plunged in grief. She seemed to have become more substantial since the death of her detestable spouse. Her hair was fluffed out, she seemed to have put on weight; her eyes were bright and her hands were steady.

'I can't say that I really care for cocktails,' she observed to Phryne. 'But Tadeusz makes really unusual ones.'

Phryne, wondering if any of her back teeth were still attached, could only nod.

Lin took his usual small glass of sherry from Hinchcliff, who seemed to be relieved. The burden of care, which had made him resemble a Presbyterian Minister about to rebuke sin, had lifted from him, and he now looked like one of those rosy-cheeked and benevolent bishops who handed out dispensations like confetti in the days before Luther had taken all the fun out of religion.

Phryne wondered what on earth the Major had had on a respectable character like Hinchcliff. She resolved to find out, solely for her own satisfaction.

'Well, children, it's time to tell all,' she said lightly. 'We have to share our secrets, my dears. If we all know the dirt on each other no one will dare to gossip. It's our only protection. Secrets have been popping out of the woodwork all over Cave House. I have to know, Miss Medenham – what on earth did the Major know about you?'

Cynthia Medenham giggled. Jack Lucas and Gerald, who seemed very well-scrubbed, came in at this point and sat down, collecting one of the Slavic cocktails each.

'It's not a very bad secret. Only, my stock in trade is mystery. The vamp, you know. Writers sell their personalities just as much as their prose. It would ruin it all to know that I've got a dear, uninteresting accountant husband and two delightful children, wouldn't it? It's true. I don't know how he found out, but he knew. He even tried to drag me into his bed, the beast – but then I got together with Letty. I led him on as shamelessly as I could – you saw me – priceless, wasn't it? A truly awful display. Then I let him take me up to his room, quite sure of his conquest. I stayed near the door, and there was – you know – a little intimacy, and then . . .'

'Then?' asked Lin, Phryne, both Fletchers, Miss Mead, Jack, Gerald, the poet and the Doctor, breathlessly.

'He got quite passionate, the monster,' said Miss Medenham with delicacy. 'And I just pointed my finger at it, you know, and I laughed. And I kept on laughing. I laughed myself out of his room and then I ran for my life back to Letty. She was staying with me. God knows what he would have done with her if she'd been there.'

Mrs Luttrell knew and shuddered. Tadeusz put an arm around her.

'That's what sent him off into the night,' observed Phryne. 'There had to be a precipitating incident. Of course, after you rejected him, he ran to the one woman he had totally under his control. Completely obedient, of course, because she was dead.'

'Poor Lina,' said the company. There was a moment's silence.

'Miss Fletcher, for you it was being seduced by the exceptionally seductive Gerald.' Miss Fletcher blushed but did not look unduly ashamed.

'Wanted to find out what it's like – what I'd be missing if I lived alone. No offence to you, Gerry dear, but it's not much.'

'No offence taken, old thing,' said Gerry cheerfully.

'And he could have blackmailed me, of course, knowing that Lin Chung is my lover. That also applied to him in reverse, if you know what I mean,' said Phryne, swapping revelation for revelation. 'Tadeusz, what was in those cocktails? They're scrambling my syntax. Let's go on. The Major had Tom over a whole cellarful of barrels because he knew that Ronald had returned and was demanding money – all he had to do to keep Tom quiet was to mention the name. He didn't need to silence Miss Mead, she wasn't in sight, but he probably would have found something.'

'Yes, dear, I have a dreadful secret,' said Miss Mead cheerfully. 'I'm a private detective. I came here to investigate Miss Cray. A very wealthy woman is thinking of donating her estate to the Church, and her lawyer could not find out which denomination Miss Cray supported.'

'You're a private detective, Miss Mead? How thrilling!' said Miss Fletcher. 'Do you have a gun, like Miss Fisher?'

'No, Miss Fletcher, I prefer to avoid any violence, though I have been unlucky today. I don't advertise and I work only for selected clients. But if my neighbours in South Yarra knew, the Lord knows what they would say. It's not difficult, you know,' she added to Miss Fletcher. 'No one notices old ladies. All I had to do to find out most of what I needed to know was to sit here in this very comfortable chair, get on with my crochet and listen.'

'Bravo, Miss Mead!' Jack Lucas was a little elevated on his first cocktail.

'Mrs Fletcher, you wasted your daughter's money but that's over now and need not attract any more notice,' said Phryne. 'But you, Tadeusz –

Ted – how long did it take you to acquire that beautiful accent?'

'How did you rumble me?' demanded the poet in a clipped tone, which lapsed back into his usual honey-sweet voice.

'I didn't for a long time. You seemed to be taken with Miss Medenham – protective colouration, I assume, for both of you. Miss Medenham had to conceal the fact that she was not having an affair, despite being one of literature's most notorious vamps, and you had to hide your interest in Letty Luttrell. But you offered me a cigarette from that battered silver case. You've obviously had it for a long time, it's personal to you, and it still has the outline of the Australian Army badge on it. Why didn't you come back to Letty, after you didn't die in the Great War?'

'I was in the cavalry, as you have surmised, and they took away our horses and sent us to the Dardanelles,' he said. 'It was butchery. I was wounded, the only one of my trench to survive a night attack. The others were all dead. I was captured. Because they thought I might have some useful information, they kept me alive. Not so much alive as to be happy, but alive enough. When they found that I didn't know what they needed, they sent me to a prison camp. There were no Empire soldiers there, but a miscellany of Russians, Poles, Hungarians and Turkish criminals. I fared badly for a while – I had been shot twice in the head and my mind was confused. I forgot who I was and where I came from. I did not even remember that I was a soldier. The camp was for criminals and illegal aliens. One of the Hungarians took to me, nursed me like a mother, and taught me words in his own language. I learned fast, because I was like a child again. You do not believe me?' Phryne looked sceptical. He took her hand and laid it on his head. 'Feel for the scars. One across the temple and behind the ear, one here, where the bullet still is. No one has dared to try and remove it.'

Phryne felt a lump over the temporal lobe, hard under her touch. Someone had certainly shot him at some time.

'So when the War was over, I forged some Hungarian papers. I had no clue to my identity. I had arrived at the camp naked in a blanket with an envelope full of meaningless trinkets. They repatriated my friend Han and me to Buda, which we found a cold city, so we went to Poland, and that is when he began to call me Tadeusz, because the name meant something to me. It is, of course, similar to Ted.'

'When did you get an idea who you were?' asked Phryne.

'Not for a long time. I wandered the world, never finding a place where I knew that I belonged. Han was a poet, but also a rich man – most unusual – and when he died he left me his estate. I turned it into gold and started to search, for I knew I had a home somewhere. Then, in London, I heard two men talking and knew the accent. They were Australians. In my little bag which I wore around my neck was a cigarette case with a regimental badge which no one in Europe had been able to identify for me. A number was scratched under it and I realised that it must be a soldier's identification.

'I went into Australia House, asked for the records, and found out that I was Private Ted Matthews, who had died in the Dardanelles campaign seven years before.

'I went back to my hotel near the British Museum and began to remember my own language, my home, and Letty. There and then I resolved to find out what had become of her. English flooded back to me, but now I spoke it like a Hungarian. I had made many friends among the surrealists, had some reputation as a poet, and I was wealthy enough to follow my own inclinations. So I came back to Australia. Letty's mother would not tell me where she was, just that she was married and happy, so I tried to forget her. I never forgot her face. Even when I was no one I saw her face, but she had no name.

'So, I had been writing poetry which is soon to be a book, if I can ever get it finished. I came here to complete the work. And Major Luttrell brought his wife here. That is the unbelievable thing, unbelievable, making me wonder if even an adopted Hungarian or Pole is under the special protection of St Stanislaus. Major Luttrell brought his wife, my Letty, here. She knew me after a few days. How did you know me, my own?' he asked, and Mrs Luttrell, nestling shamelessly against him, said, 'Your eyes, Ted. I knew your eyes.'

'We were going to run away together,' resumed the poet, 'though that would bring my Letty into social disrepute. We met in the library. I left messages for her there. We were counting on the ineffable Cynthia to distract him sufficiently so that we could make what I believe is called a clean getaway, hmm? However, now the Major is dead and this fortunately is not necessary. Another cocktail, if you please.'

'What a story!' exclaimed Miss Fletcher. Phryne, reserving her opinion on the likelihood of this romantic history, rose and stretched. If Letty believed it, who was she to cavil?

'Well, that's all the mysteries but two. Hinchcliff, can you bring Doreen in here?'

The Butler's eyebrows left his control and rose, slightly. He bowed and went out.

Miss Medenham wound up the gramophone. Mr and Mrs Reynolds came in and sat down. Evelyn had cried herself out, washed her face, and looked composed and sad, but not heartbroken. Her boy was dead. Now she could bury him, and mourn.

Tom Reynolds, bulkier than ever with bandages across his shoulder and chest, accepted a cocktail against competent medical advice and swigged it. This took his breath so comprehensively that he could only goggle as a weeping chambermaid was ushered in by the butler.

'Doreen, you left the urns,' said Phryne gently. 'It had to be you. Only you could get into all the rooms without being noticed. You knew Lina's body was in the Buchan Caves. How did you know?'

Doreen burst into tears and was supplied with a glass of sherry and a handkerchief.

'He told me,' she finally managed. 'The Major. He knew about everyone. He knew about Annie's babies. He got Mr H in debt to him for hundreds of pounds, gambling on those wicked cards. He knew about me and Mr Jones, he threatened to tell Madam and get me fired, and I've got five sisters, I can't go home. He didn't want to ... to ... he didn't want me in that way. It would have been easier if he did. He just wanted to talk to me. He liked to come to the kitchen window and boast about it – about the girls he'd strangled in India, about his wife being next after me if I told on him, about Lina and where he'd put her. He said he'd kill me if I told. So I left the urns for you, Miss Fisher, you being so clever and all. Oh, dear.' She wept with relief into Lin Chung's silk handkerchief.

'It was very brave of you to try and help me,' said Phryne.

'It's all right, Doreen, I'm not going to dismiss you,' said Mrs Reynolds wearily. 'You go back to the kitchen now, and ask Cook for some hot tea.'

Doreen snuffled, blew her nose, and went out.

Phryne felt a gentle hand on her arm. It was the beautiful Gerald, rosy and angelic, smiling his guileless child's smile.

'You promised,' he reminded her.

'Oh, yes, so I did. It's all fixed. Tom, can I take Jack to pick out his paintings now?' she called. Mr Reynolds assented, and she took Jack Lucas and his lover into the corridor.

'Paintings?' he exclaimed. 'There isn't anything in this house worth having. It's all etchings of the Monarch of the Glen and pretty little pastels done by ladies which look like endive salad, dying. What have you sold my birthright for, eh?'

'Trust me,' said Phryne crossly. 'And follow me,' she added, making her best pace up the stairs to the room which had been the Major's.

'The builders of Cave House went on a Grand Tour,' she told Lucas, opening the door.

'I know, that's where they got that near-Boucher and all those naughty prints of naked ladies,' snapped Jack Lucas. 'None of it worth more than threepence-ha'penny on the open market.'

'Yes, but what else was on in Paris in the 1880s?' asked Phryne acidly, bringing the young man's nose to surface with the large oil depicting a wobbly church. He squinted. There was a silence. Then Gerald began to laugh. He reeled over, staggering and whooping with mirth, to enfold Phryne in a close embrace, weeping tears of joy down her neck and kissing her gleefully between paroxysms.

'You mean ... from the Salon des Refusés?' said Jack. 'Yes, there's the signature ... It's a Manet, a genuine Manet ... My God, why have I never seen these before?'

'You have spent insufficient time in servants'

bedrooms. In my chamber is what I judge to be a Monet; there's a very pretty little Renoir of a girl with an umbrella in Lina's room and a swingeing great expanse of grass and lilies which have to be either Pissarro or possibly very early Sisley in the servants' hall. Impeccable provenance, by the way – the original bills of sale are in the library. I asked Tom for ten of them and he agreed. It seems that both he and his wife don't like all this modern stuff, so they put them away out of the public eye. I think they ought to realise you enough for a nice comfortable life, don't you? Or would you rather go and argue with Tom Reynolds for your thousand pounds?'

'Miss Fisher, these are worth thousands, we can't accept . . .' began Jack and Gerald cried out in protest.

Phryne said, 'Yes, you can. Tom knows, more or less, what these are worth. But he was very close friends with your father and only his own stubbornness stopped him from giving you cash. This terribly generous gift assuages his conscience and he'll be very hurt if you don't take them. Don't, by the way, miss the tiny little Seurat of an acrobat in Doreen's room. It's a gem. Now, for God's sake, escort me to the dining room. It's been an interesting day and I'd like a glass or two of wine.'

Gerald and Jack held out an arm each, and Phryne paraded down the monumental stair between two beautiful young men. They made an impressive entrance into dinner.

Dinner was lavish, if scrappily served, the kitchen being still deeply engrossed in enough gossip to last them for years. The company adjourned to the parlour to repair their ravelled nerves with dancing and conversation. The music began to play, a slow foxtrot, ideal for the sleepy end of a dreadful day. Tadeusz drew Mrs Luttrell to her feet, saying, 'If you dance with me I'll do the bravest thing man ever did for woman.'

'Oh, what's that?' asked Letty, nestling into his arms. The dark-brown hair flopped over his forehead and she smoothed it back. Tadeusz assumed a grave demeanour.

'I'll go and teach Mrs Croft how to make coffee,' he said solemnly and Letty laughed.

Miss Medenham snared the Doctor. Miss Fletcher was claimed by Gerald and Mrs Fletcher danced with Jack. Phryne reflected irritably that Cave House seemed to be positively oozing with happy endings.

Lin openly escorted Miss Fisher to her room. Dot, full of tea and gossip, had gone to bed. The murdered girl and the death of the murderers would not be banished from Phryne's mind, and the slow inexorable fall insisted on unrolling itself before her tired eyes like a motion picture. She sat down at the table to remove her makeup, and an open book caught her eye. *Urne Buriall*, by the very learned Sir Thomas Browne.

Afflictions induce calloufities; miferies are

slippery or fall like snow upon us, which nonwithftanding is no unhappy stupidity. To be ignorant of evils to come, and forgetful of evils paft, is merciful provifion in nature, whereby we digest the mixture of our few and evil days and, our delivered senfes not relapsing into cutting remembrances, our sorrows are not kept raw by the edge of repetitions.

Phryne puzzled through the unfamiliar spelling, nodded soberly, and stood up into Lin Chung's arms.